"You didn't answer my question about the festival. Will you go with me?"

"And show you the *real* Bayou de Joie?" Brianne said. "Like the pirate Lafitte's hideout, the tavern where he and his men sat, drank, and planned their next raid, and maybe even where he supposedly hid his treasure?"

Mace shrugged. "That, and perhaps where an eager Californian can take a Southern lady to lunch and get to know her a little better."

"What kind of business are you in, exactly?" she asked, suddenly wanting to know more about this man who was causing a myriad of conflicting emotions to speed through her body.

"Investments," he said. "And you're avoiding the subject of being my guide."

"I have other guests to see to. And work to do."

Mace reached out and touched her hand, brushing his fingers lightly down its side.

Brianne shivered and looked up at him, but she didn't pull away.

She felt his hand move lightly up the length of her arm, felt his fingers, warm and strong, settle around her flesh. His breath danced over her cheek as he neared, a soul-touching caress that left her aching for more.

He was going to kiss her.

WHAT ARE *LOVESWEPT* ROMANCES?

They are stories of true romance and touching emotion. We believe those two very important ingredients are constants in our highly sensual and very believable stories in the LOVESWEPT line. Our goal is to give you, the reader, stories of consistently high quality that may sometimes make you laugh, sometimes make you cry, but are always fresh and creative and contain many delightful surprises within their pages.

Most romance fans read an enormous number of books. Those they truly love, they keep. Others may be traded with friends and soon forgotten. We hope that each LOVESWEPT romance will be a treasure—a "keeper." We will always try to publish

LOVE STORIES YOU'LL NEVER FORGET
BY AUTHORS YOU'LL ALWAYS REMEMBER

The Editors

NEVER ALONE

CHERYLN BIGGS

BANTAM BOOKS
NEW YORK · TORONTO · LONDON · SYDNEY · AUCKLAND

NEVER ALONE
A Bantam Book / June 1998

LOVESWEPT *and the wave design are registered trademarks of Bantam Books, a division of Bantam Doubleday Dell Publishing Group, Inc. Registered in U.S. Patent and Trademark Office and elsewhere.*

All rights reserved.
Copyright © 1998 by Cheryln Biggs.
Cover art copyright © 1998 by Aleta Jenks.
No part of this book may be reproduced or transmitted in any form or by any means, electronic or mechanical, including photocopying, recording, or by any information storage and retrieval system, without permission in writing from the publisher.
For information address: Bantam Books.

If you purchased this book without a cover you should be aware that this book is stolen property. It was reported as "unsold and destroyed" to the publisher and neither the author nor the publisher has received any payment for this "stripped book."

ISBN 0-553-44640-1

Published simultaneously in the United States and Canada

Bantam Books are published by Bantam Books, a division of Bantam Doubleday Dell Publishing Group, Inc. Its trademark, consisting of the words "Bantam Books" and the portrayal of a rooster, is Registered in U.S. Patent and Trademark Office and in other countries. Marca Registrada. Bantam Books, 1540 Broadway, New York, New York 10036.

PRINTED IN THE UNITED STATES OF AMERICA

OPM   10 9 8 7 6 5 4 3 2 1

This book is dedicated with love
to all the men of history whose
legends have become larger than life,
but most especially to four of my
all-time favorites:
Athos, Aramis, Porthos, and
D'Artagnan.
The world became a richer place
because you were in it.
It would become richer still if only
you could come back.
May your spirits revel in adventure
. . . wherever you are.

Dear Reader,

When I was asked to write a special note to you to be included with my book, I didn't know what to write. I thought about it and even started writing several times, only to erase everything. Then I decided to ask Aramis.

By now I'm sure you're thinking, Oh, dear, she really is crazy!

No, I'm not. It's just that we writers have characters running around in our minds yelling at us to tell their stories, and sometimes even after we do, they hang around awhile.

Never Alone was a very special story for me, so my four handsome friends will stay with me for a very long time, probably hoping, or arrogantly expecting, that I'll write another story around them.

Anyway, they *all* decided to put their two cents in on this note.

First, **Athos** gallantly suggested that I thank you, which I thought was a wonderful idea. So, thank you for buying my books and liking them. Years ago if someone had told me I would be a published author, my books would be in stores, and I would receive fan letters, I would have declared *them* crazy. But here I am, and I have saved every wonderful letter ever written to me.

D'Artagnan suggested since this book is included in an anniversary month I share what anniversaries mean to me. Each year my wedding anniversary marks another year I have spent with a man I love very much. We went through a lot of hard times in order to be together, but they were well worth it . . . because we did end up together.

Porthos blustered, naturally, that I expound on the musketeers, their gallantry, chivalry, bravery—but that's enough of that. Years ago I read the book *The Three Musketeers*, by Alexandre Dumas, then saw the movie with Oliver Reed. I liked it. Then a few years ago the movie was remade with Kiefer Sutherland, Charlie Sheen, Oliver Platt, and Chris O'Donnell. It made me laugh, cry, chuckle, and swoon. It was as these four swashbuckled their way across the screen and through history that I fell in love with the Musketeers and knew someday I would have to include them in one of my stories.

When my wonderful editor invited me to participate in this special month of Loveswepts and suggested a ghost story, my heart leaped, because I knew exactly what I was going to write. It was their time, and a fun time they did give me along the way.

Many people believe that the four Musketeers were merely fictional characters made up by Alexandre Dumas in his best-loved books. Dumas played with history, changing facts, events, and circumstances here and there, yet many threads of truth are woven through his stories. One of those truths is that the four Musketeers, Aramis, Athos, Porthos, and D'Artagnan, were indeed real men who swore to protect their king, and donned the uniform of his elite company of guards, the musketeers.

Then **Aramis** finally spoke his mind. "Give them your opinion of an extraordinary lover," he said, puffing his chest out and smiling wickedly.

Leave it to him to suggest that, I thought, and laughed. I just as quickly sobered. An extraordinary lover. How would I describe such a man? Then I smiled, because I knew.

In my opinion an extraordinary lover is the man who holds you in his arms when you feel sad and promises that everything will be all right; waits on you hand and foot when you're sick; brings you your favorite dessert every night just because he knows you love it; takes care of all the animals you insist on adopting because . . . though you love having them around, you hate the drudgery of feeding them. He is the man who goes to the mall with you and doesn't complain when you can't make up your mind what to buy, who occupies himself in a bookstore waiting for you to gather your purchases, takes you to a movie you're dying to see but he knows he'll hate, listens to your gripes, worries, and whining, and then sympathizes and holds out his arms to you. An extraordinary lover is the man who makes the commitment to love you, cherish you, and take care of you for the rest of his life . . . and means it.

I wish you all an Extraordinary Lover,

Cherylyn Biggs

PROLOGUE

LeiMonte Castle, France
Summer 1987

"*En garde!*" Porthos raised his sword and lunged at the approaching workman.

The man walked right through him.

Porthos spun, staring at the workman's retreating back. "Coward!" He slashed his sword through the air, then turned on his heel and looked at his cohorts. "How in the devil are we supposed to fight them when they keep walking through us?"

"Perhaps we should pray instead," Aramis suggested. As he made the sign of the cross, the gold ring he wore, its onyx-and-diamond-encrusted face depicting the Musketeers insignia, sparkled brilliantly.

"*Bon Dieu,*" Porthos snapped. "Pray! Hah!" He slashed the air with his sword again. "Praying hasn't done you a lick of good in the past three hundred and fifty years, so why think that will change now?"

Athos, lounging on one of the marble garden benches the workmen had yet to load onto their truck, savored a drink of his favorite wine, and sighed. "Calm yourself, my friend." He draped an arm over his raised knee, the lace-edged cuff of his shirt dangling down over his knuckles. "I sincerely doubt there is anything we can do to stop them."

"But they're packing up our damned castle," Porthos shrieked. "Or what's left of it." He turned abruptly, and as the silver threads of the fleur-de-lis embroidered on his musketeer's cloak caught the sun, he glared at the only one of them who hadn't said a word in the last hour. "Well, D'Artagnan, what have you to say? Do we stand here and do nothing while they cart off our home?"

D'Artagnan stroked absently with thumb and forefinger at the small, dark goatee on his chin as a thoughtful frown drew at his brow. He shook his head, then turned away from studying the workmen and looked at his old friend. "Porthos, do you remember where your coffin was buried?"

Porthos sputtered. "My coffin?" He looked around, puzzled. "No."

D'Artagnan nodded. "It was placed in the west wall of the main floor."

Porthos slid his sword into its elaborately scrolled scabbard and threw up his hands in frustration. "Wonderful. So you remembered where I was buried. Congratulations."

"Where we were all buried," D'Artagnan corrected.

Porthos screwed up his round face. "At the moment I don't see the point or the importance of that." He glanced over his shoulder as one of the men started his truck. The sound of the rumbling engine destroyed the valley's silence. "They're about to take our home."

"And us along with it," D'Artagnan added.

ONE

LeiMonte Castle
Bayou de Joie on Barataria Bay, Louisiana
Summer 1997

Brianne hung up the phone and smacked a hand down on her desk. "Damn."

"Something wrong?"

She looked up at hearing her uncle enter the study, which she also used as an office whenever she worked at home. "The Pilgrimage Society overbooked us."

Felix St. John crossed the room toward her, his cane clacking on the hardwood floor with each step. The black silk lapel of his red velvet smoking jacket shimmered in the afternoon sun that flowed into the room through the windows behind Brianne's desk. "Put them in the Tower Room. It's empty."

Brianne shifted in the high-backed chair that had once belonged to Anne of Austria and stared up at her uncle, unable to believe what he'd suggested. "Oh, right," she said, and threw him a mocking glare. "Put them in the Tower Room. If you'll remember, the last time we put someone up there, we had to call the paramedics."

Felix laughed, though the sound that rattled through his deceptively frail-looking old body and escaped his lips sounded more like a gargling cackle. "Well, it wasn't as if Porthos didn't offer that old stuffed shirt a sporting chance."

"He wasn't old or a stuffed shirt," Brianne said. "Anyway, having someone you can't see cause a whirlwind in your room, slice up your best suit, grab a sword off the wall, and throw it at you is not my idea of a sporting chance, Uncle Felix."

He laughed again, took a book from one of the shelves, then looked back at Brianne. "He didn't throw it at him, Brianne, and you know it. He tossed it to him, handle first, like a gentleman. And it was a challenge. Anyway, it's not their fault no one but you and I can hear or see them, you know. I imagine it must get very frustrating for them at times."

"But that's all the more reason for them to behave when we have guests."

Felix shook his head, causing a thick lock of snow-white hair to fall onto his temple. "You have to remember, honey, this was their home first."

"A fact which they make certain we don't forget." She glanced at the life-size portrait of the famous Musketeers that hung over the fireplace mantel, then looked toward the door. "So, speaking of our four devils, where are they now?"

Felix shrugged. "Haven't seen them all day, but I'm sure they're around."

"Oh, I'm sure," Brianne quipped.

A loud crashing sound suddenly reverberated through the house.

Brianne stood. "We really should install some soft chimes, Uncle Felix. That brass knocker sounds like trees falling in the foyer."

"It is a historically authentic detail," her uncle said.

She knew what was coming next.

"So it stays."

"Fine, but if one of our guests has a heart attack someday after being scared witless by the sound of that thing, don't say I didn't warn you."

The brass door knocker slammed against its plate again before she was halfway through the foyer, and she cringed.

Mace Calder stared at the elegant brass knocker and wondered for the hundredth time what in blazes he was doing in Bayou de Joie, Louisiana. Hot, humid, tourist-crowded Bayou de Joie on Barataria Bay, Louisiana. He slid a hand impatiently through his black hair and ignored the slightly distorted reflection of himself that stared back at him from the door knocker's brilliantly polished plate.

Of course, he knew all too well what he was doing there. Or what he intended to do. Donald J. Melanstrup was Mace's client—his most important client—and after two weeks of information gathering, Mace had come to realize that to carry out Melanstrup's instructions, he had to engage in some hands-on investigating, which meant a personal visit to LeiMonte Castle.

But he also had to be discreet, which was why he'd told the woman at the Pilgrimage Society that he was merely a businessman there on vacation.

He sighed. Was anyone ever going to answer the door?

A loud, spine-tingling screech suddenly pierced the air. Mace jerked around, half expecting to see some kind of crazed swamp-thing-she-monster barreling toward him. Instead, he stared into the round, beady eye of a peacock as it cocked its head to one side and stared back. The bird stood a few feet away, its colorful tail feathers spread majestically, its royal-blue body feathers glistening brilliantly in the waning sun.

"Figures," he mumbled. The inhabitants of LeiMonte Castle obviously didn't have watchdogs, they had watch peacocks.

Mace turned back and contemplated using the door knocker again.

Perhaps if his day hadn't proven to be one problem after another right from the start, he wouldn't be in such a surly mood. First the limo he'd taken to the airport that morning had suffered a flat tire on the way. Then he'd encountered a delay with his flight out of San Francisco. Another delay in changing planes had greeted him upon arriving in Dallas. He hadn't had time to reserve a car in New Orleans ahead of time, so he'd had to settle for a sleek red sports car convertible from the rental agency. Personally he loved it. Professionally he knew it was better to remain low-key, which was why he usually reserved an economy sedan.

When he'd finally arrived at the Pilgrimage Society's headquarters in Bayou de Joie to pick up the registration packet for his stay at LeiMonte, he found there had been a problem with his room reservation. Luckily they'd been able to work that out, but if he'd been a superstitious person, he might have begun to think someone was trying to tell him to forget about this deal.

Mace almost snorted aloud at the thought.

Thankfully he wasn't superstitious, and even if he were, this deal, if he could pull it off, promised to be much too lucrative to walk away from, no matter what he had to go through to get it completed.

He grasped the knocker. It would be nice, however, if someone—someday—would answer the blasted door of this monstrosity that had been described as a French castle. Mace pounded the knocker soundly.

A second later he heard footsteps echo from the interior of the place. "Finally!"

Halfway through the foyer Brianne stopped short as a flash of white scooted across the floor, nearly tripping her. She regained her balance and glared at the cat that bounded gracefully up the grand staircase. It was a good thing Serendipity wasn't black, or Brianne would probably have had about five years of bad luck in store for her, and Serendipity would most likely have gone through about seven of her nine lives.

"Coming, coming," the housekeeper called brightly from the rear of the house.

Brianne paused and looked over her shoulder as the woman waddled into the great hall, wiping flour-covered hands on her apron.

"I thought you were still at the market, Mrs. Peel."

The housekeeper smiled and waved a pudgy hand at Brianne as she neared, then tucked a stray strand of hair back into the silver-gray braid atop her head. "Oh, dear me, no, child. I've been back forever."

"Well, you look busy. I'll get the door. You go on back to whatever it is you're doing."

"Making pecan pies," Mrs. Peel said, a twinkle in her blue eyes as she grinned. "Mr. St. John's favorite." She turned and disappeared toward the kitchen.

Brianne smiled to herself. If it wasn't for the fact that Mrs. Peel was married to John, their gardener, she would have sworn long ago that the older woman was in love with Felix.

The knocker sounded again and Brianne jumped, having momentarily forgotten about the person still standing on the porch. Most probably it was the guest the society had called her about. She cursed softly as the annoying sound of the knocker faded away and wished again that her uncle would relent on the idea of getting chimes.

Her reflection in the mirror that hung over a petticoat table set against one wall of the foyer caught her attention as she started to pass, and Brianne paused to give herself a quick once-over. Her long hair could use a brushing, her cheeks were flushed, and her lipstick was worn off. "Along with my good mood," she mumbled as the sound of the infernal door knocker crashed down around her again.

She ran to the door and grabbed its knob.

TWO

Mace heard the click of the doorknob and bent to retrieve his garment bag and briefcase, which he'd set down near the tall door before knocking. An hour or so ago? he thought wryly. Straightening as the huge door swung open, he found himself looking into the deepest pair of gray-blue eyes he'd ever seen, and feeling as if someone had just sucker punched him.

The face that went with those mesmerizing eyes was not classically beautiful by any stretch of the imagination. It was not one that would ever grace the cover of a fashion magazine for fashion's sake alone, yet it was arresting, a cross somewhere between a royal princess and an impish pixie, totally exotic, unreasonably captivating. Mace was momentarily mesmerized.

"Welcome to LeiMonte," the woman said.

Mace quickly regrouped and clamped a lid on

the wayward, erotic thoughts that had instantly shot to mind as his gaze swept over her. He cleared his throat and reminded himself why he was there. He required all his energies, all his concentration for Melanstrup's deal. He could take care of his libido some other time.

Nevertheless, the thought didn't prevent his gaze from moving over her again, a little more slowly this time. The pictures he'd seen of her hadn't done her justice.

Mace hadn't had time to develop a complete case file before coming to LeiMonte, because Melanstrup was in such a hurry. But he did know quite a bit about Felix St. John, or at least as much as he needed. Getting information on the octogenarian had been simple. He was one of the most prominent old-timers left in Louisiana. But Mace had only been able to gather the bare facts about the man's grandniece.

She obviously cherished her privacy a lot more than her uncle did his.

As Mace's eyes devoured her appreciatively his mind clicked over the facts he knew about her.

Brianne St. John's parents had died sixteen years earlier, leaving their ten-year-old daughter to be cared for by Felix, a widower with no children of his own, and the sole owner of one of the nation's largest shipping companies, among other things. He'd sent her to the best schools, and after college she'd come back and gone straight to work for St. John Shipping. Now Felix was eighty, had recently retired and appointed Brianne to take over the running of the company. Not bad for a little grandniece.

She wasn't what Mace had expected. A young Joan Crawford. Bette Davis. Even Barbara Stanwyck. That's the type he'd expected. Hard. Cold. All business. But the woman standing before him now was quite the opposite. Brianne St. John's eyes were too soft and deep to be deemed hard or cold. Her nose was too pert, her lips too sensuous, her red-gold hair too rich and tempting. And she had curves in all the right places.

That last assessment instantly put ideas in Mace's head that had no business being there. He mentally shook himself and exerted the iron-will control that had enabled him not only to climb the corporate ladder, but reach its top. As quickly and thoroughly as a chameleon changes his color, a cold mantle of aloofness settled onto his features and into his demeanor. "Well, I was beginning to think there was no one here," he said curtly.

Brianne stared, momentarily taken aback first by his looks, then by his brusque words. The man was one of the most attractive she'd ever seen, in a hard-edged, roguish sort of way, but his manners obviously left a lot to be desired. It hadn't taken her *that* long to answer his incessant knockings.

"I'm Mace Calder. I have a reservation."

She felt as if he expected her to curtsy. Instead, she bit back the tart retort that burned on her tongue and reminded herself that he was a guest,

Never Alone

and she was supposed to be the gracious hostess. After all, it was festival time in the South, which meant one should ooze with chivalry and hospitality, even if they were forced. Brianne compelled a smile to her lips. "Yes, Mr. Calder, we've been expecting you. I'm Brianne St. John."

She stepped back, opening the door wider in welcome. "Please, come in."

His cologne, resembling the subtle scents of a night-shrouded desert, teased her nose as he moved past her across the threshold. She stared after him. Over six feet tall, piercing dark blue eyes, straight and slightly mussed hair glinting blue-black in the sunlight, a nose that was long, straight, and slightly flared at the end, a square jaw that, she sensed, could come to resemble a slash of granite when he was angry, and well-defined lips. It was an extremely strong face. Not aristocratically handsome, but virilely handsome.

A cool breeze brushed across Brianne's shoulder and rippled softly through her long hair.

"Tsk, tsk. Do I detect more than a bit of interest in that assessing once-over you're giving this young man, milady?"

She threw a glowering glance over her shoulder as Porthos chuckled.

"No, you do not!" she whispered hastily.

"Pardon me?" Mace turned back to her as he set his bags down.

Brianne flushed. "Oh, ah, nothing."

He looked at her queerly. She had definitely said something. He'd heard her.

"I'm not certain he is the type for you," D'Artagnan said, stepping up to her other side and giving Mace his own brand of once-over. "Looks a bit shifty."

She ignored them both. "Welcome to Bayou de Joie and LeiMonte Castle, Mr. Calder. I hope you didn't have any trouble finding us."

"No, none."

Brianne watched him as he looked around the reception hall, glanced at the ceiling two stories above and the huge brass chandelier that hung from it.

If he felt the ghosts' presence, he didn't show it. But then, she'd never met anyone yet who had felt, seen, or heard them, so there really was no cause to wonder at all.

"Interesting place." He reached into the inside pocket of the lightweight leather sport coat he wore, pulled out the Pilgrimage Society's registration packet, and handed it to her.

His warm fingers brushed against hers as she took it.

Brianne's hand trembled. She quickly pulled away from him and opened the packet, telling herself she was merely nervous about having to tell him about the Tower Room. The problem was, what was she going to tell him? She stared at the confirmation slip.

"I understand there was some problem with my

reservation," Mace said, as if reading her thoughts. "I assume I do have a room."

"Yes," Brianne said, refolding the paper and slipping it back into its envelope. "But there is something about the room that I should tell you, Mr. Calder. Something you should know before you decide to . . . well, you see, there's a problem. . . ."

"A problem," Mace echoed, not in the mood for another annoyance.

"Yes, well, it's not so much a problem as it is a bother."

"Bother?" Porthos shrieked, his face popping up before hers. "We're a *bother*?"

She forced herself not to acknowledge him or respond to his outburst.

Mace stared at her. "What kind of bother, Miss St. John?"

"Well, it's just that . . ." How was she supposed to tell him? He'd think she was crazy, and Porthos was likely to go off the deep end if she was too . . . accurate. Brianne smacked the reservation packet he'd handed her lightly against her thigh. Her agreement with the Pilgrimage Society forbid her to turn away a guest who had preregistered through them—even if it meant putting him in the Tower Room. So, unless she wanted to jeopardize the castle's standing as a guest residence, which she knew Felix didn't want to do—he didn't need the money, but he loved showing off his castle—she had no choice but to tell this guest the truth and hope for the best. "Well, what I mean . . ."

Mace looked down at her, then sighed in frustration.

Brianne felt her fingers tremble. Why did she suddenly feel so nervous?

"So which is it, Miss St. John? Do I have a room here or not?"

"Yes, you do, if you want it. But I must explain; the Pilgrimage Society overbooked us," she said in a rush of words, "and I'm afraid the only accommodation I have left is the Tower Room."

Mace shrugged. "So I'll take the Tower Room. A few stairs won't kill me."

"It's not the stairs, Mr. Calder."

"No, it's not the stairs, Mr. Calder," Porthos said, and laughed.

"Stop it," Brianne snapped, and slapped a hand toward Porthos.

"Excuse me?" Mace frowned. "Stop what?"

Driving me crazy, Brianne thought. But the silent comment wasn't meant for Mace Calder. "I'm sorry, I didn't mean you, Mr. Calder. I was batting at a very bothersome little insect."

"Now I'm an insect?" Porthos said.

Brianne waved a hand in front of her face again, as if in evidence of her words, then looked back at the new guest and spoke before she could change her mind and send him packing. "The Tower Room is haunted."

His gaze remained pinned on her, but his look was blank.

"I said it's—"

"I know what you said," Mace retorted, cutting her off.

A sardonic smile pulled at one corner of his mouth, and Brianne had the uneasy feeling she'd seen that devilish grin somewhere before. But of course that was ridiculous, since she knew she'd never met Mace Calder.

"The room is haunted," Mace said, repeating her words. "But I was under the impression the entire place was supposed to be haunted."

"Well, yes, that's true, but they don't usually bother with the other bedrooms. The Tower Room, though, is special. It's where . . ." She glanced at Porthos, still standing nearby, arms crossed over his wide chest as he watched her. His smug smile poked at her temper. She looked back at Mace. "It's where they used to meet." And still did, she added silently, remembering the card game they'd indulged in two weeks before, which had resulted in Mrs. Peel having to painstakingly glue an antique vase back together, repair a sword's slash through the drapes, and toss out the small table they'd been using.

"Where they used to meet," Mace echoed flatly.

"Yes."

"Who?"

"The Musketeers."

Mace sighed. This was the woman who was running St. John Shipping? He was starting to find that fact hard to believe. Maybe she was just a figurehead. "Fine," he said. "Which way?"

"If you take the room, Mr. Calder, it is at your own risk," she added, not willing to have to pay for another damaged suit, or worse.

Mace nodded. He had planned to be the epitome of cordiality and grace, even seductiveness if necessary. But he was too tired, too frustrated, and just in too bad a mood at the moment to worry that he was probably coming across more like Grumpy than Cary Grant. He certainly wasn't going to be frightened away from LeiMonte by some ridiculous ghost story. This deal was too important.

His dark eyes met hers. "I don't believe in ghosts, Miss St. John. Nor do I believe in the bogeyman, vampires, witches, werewolves, zombies, walking mummies, or things that go bump in the night."

"Well, he sounds like fun," Porthos said with a sneer.

"So I don't think your ghosts are going to bother me," Mace finished.

Brianne ignored Porthos and stiffened at the condescension she detected in Mace Calder's tone. "Fine. I'll show you to your room," she said coolly, and turned toward the stairs. "If you'll follow me?"

Mace picked up his bags and followed Brianne up the stairs. He had acted like a jerk, and he'd have to make up for it later, whether she was really involved with running the company or not. He would have to charm her. But that was later. Right now all he wanted to do was sit down, relax, make a few phone calls, and get some answers.

Then he'd know whether to follow his original strategy, or rethink it.

The sway of her hips beneath the snugly fitting black slacks she wore drew his attention as they moved up the stairs. For the second time in less than fifteen minutes, thoughts he had no business thinking filled his mind.

Worse, his body had started to react to those traitorous thoughts and that delectable composite of curves moving ahead of him.

Business, he reminded himself coldly. Business. That was the only reason he was there, the only thing he intended to pay attention to. Business. He didn't need and he didn't want a woman in his life. Not in any kind of permanent way, at least. He'd had enough to deal with ending his last relationship. He needed to keep his heels solidly on the ground and his passions cooled.

Just the thought of Stephanie Rothenberg was enough to put a damper on Mace's impulsive ardor, which is exactly what he'd intended.

Of course, if there ever came a time when thinking of Stephanie didn't work, he could pull up memories of Jaclyn Chellden. His only fear was that thinking of both those relationships at the same time might end in permanent impotency.

After traversing a long, wide hall, Brianne

turned into what looked like an alcove. To one side of it was a delicate wrought-iron staircase spiraling upward.

"I thought this was supposed to be a real European castle," Mace said as they climbed, trying to keep his mind off the long, lithe legs in front of his eyes.

"LeiMonte *is* a real European castle," Brianne retorted. "My uncle brought it over piece by piece from France about ten years ago."

"Aren't castles supposed to be made of stone, and have turrets, drawbridges, and moats?"

"Not all castles in France are like that," Brianne said. LeiMonte had been built by the Comte de la Fère as a summer residence. She opened the tower door and stepped into the room.

Soft ivory-painted walls contrasted beautifully with burgundy damask drapes.

"As I've told you before, it was actually built by my father and given to me as a wedding present," Athos said.

She glanced at the tall Musketeer whose pale blue eyes always seemed so full of haunting memories and sadness.

He shrugged. "I probably should have burned it down."

"Then where would you be now?" she whispered as she drew back the heavy drapes that covered the windows to reveal a breathtaking view of the open countryside, as well as the swamps and marshes around LeiMonte.

"France," Athos said.

She turned and looked back at Mace Calder.

He recognized the room's furnishings as authentic seventeenth-century artifacts. He also noted a slight chill in the room that was definitely cooler than the rest of the house. With a muted sigh he tossed his bags onto a canopied bed.

"Dinner will be served in the dining room in an hour," Brianne said. "Seven, every night." She walked to the door, then looked back to see if anyone, other than Mace Calder, was still in the room.

"Did you have to put him in *our* room?" D'Artagnan said as he lazed against the staircase rail.

She stepped onto the small landing that put her almost nose to nose with him and closed the Tower Room's door behind her. "I didn't have a choice," she whispered. "The society overbooked us."

D'Artagnan propped a hip onto the banister and slid down beside her as she descended the stairs. "So put him in the dungeon," he quipped. "I don't like him."

She stopped at the base of the stairs and turned to stare at him as he jumped with a graceful flourish to the floor.

Although never a really handsome man, the Musketeer was definitely distinguished-looking, with his long dark curls draping his shoulders and a look in his eyes that dared anyone to question his actions. He was the epitome of gallantry, chivalry, and everything a Musketeer should be. Unfortunately, he was also opinionated, stubborn, and had a wicked streak a mile wide.

Brianne jammed clenched fists onto her hips. "First, as you very well know, we don't have a dungeon; otherwise I might be tempted to find some way to lock you down there for a while." She struggled against the smile that pulled at the corners of her lips as his eyes grew wide with a pretense of shock. "And second, Mace Calder has been here all of ten minutes and you don't know one thing about him, so how can you say you don't like him?"

D'Artagnan shrugged. "I don't have to *know* anything about him to know I don't like him."

"Double that for me," Athos said.

She looked at the tall blond who suddenly appeared beside his darker cohort.

"And me," Porthos added.

"Definitely," Aramis chimed in, materializing beside Porthos. The mother of all devilish smiles curved his almost too perfectly carved lips.

Brianne groaned. "Don't do this."

They feigned innocent looks. "Do what?" all four said in unison.

She turned her back to them, but as she walked down the hall toward the main staircase, trying to count to ten so as not to scream, she had a sneaky feeling that a dark cloud had just descended on LeiMonte Castle.

THREE

Brianne returned to the study.

"All settled into the Tower Room?" Felix asked.

She caught the amusement in his tone and chose to ignore the question. "I need to make a call to the office and verify that the fax from Broadelay Shipping came in."

"Relax, Brianne. This is festival. I'm sure Cummings can handle the things at the office for a couple of days," Felix said.

"Ah, there you are, Miss St. John!"

Brianne and Felix both turned to look toward the open door that led to the foyer.

As Christian Deuvelle, an art dealer from France and another of their guests, strolled into the room, Brianne silently cursed herself for not shutting the door behind her when she'd entered.

To her dismay the four Musketeers strolled in on the man's heels, all smiling.

"I must say," Christian said excitedly, "you have done an excellent job restoring LeiMonte Castle. I have been wandering about upstairs and everything is absolutely extraordinary." He moved around the study as he spoke, assessing everything, his hands and arms flitting about with each word that slipped from his lips. "Everything looks so marvelously authentic."

Felix bristled. "Everything *is* marvelously authentic, Deuvelle. I would have thought, as an art dealer, you would be able to distinguish between an authentic piece and a reproduction."

"Ah, but I deal only in books and paintings, *mon ami*." He looked around the study. "Surely not all of this magnificent period furniture is authentic, monsieur?" He rushed to the windows and touched the gold-fringed blue brocade that framed them. "These are absolutely extraordinary draperies."

Brianne threw a quick glance at Felix and saw his gnarled old fingers tighten round his cane, but before she could respond to Christian Deuvelle, her uncle did.

"Of course all of the furniture and tapestries and draperies are authentic!" Felix's gray-blue eyes flashed with indignation. "Obviously, without records we could not track down the very pieces that were at LeiMonte when the Comte de la Fère lived there, but everything is authentic to the period," he barked. "Each piece was bought and imported from France the same time as the castle."

Christian glanced at Brianne and smiled. "Ah,

but certainly you must have used, ah, some reproductions to restore parts of the building that had deteriorated from neglect. Doors, windows, cornices." He shrugged. "And of course the ceiling paintings and silk wallpapers."

Brianne hurried to intervene, seeing that her uncle looked ready either to pop a vein, or use the golden alligator head that topped his cane to split the Frenchman's skull.

"Have you seen the formal gardens, Mr. Deuvelle?" she asked, turning Christian back toward the great hall. "They were designed to be exactly like they were when the king's Musketeers used the castle to thwart Cardinal Richelieu and Marie de Médicis's designs to control the throne."

The dark brown eyes that looked into hers told Brianne that Christian Deuvelle had a lot more on his mind than looking at gardens or discussing Musketeers, three-hundred-year-old power struggles, and secret meetings. "No, Mademoiselle St. John, I have not," he said softly, "but I would very much like to see the gardens, if you will be kind enough to join me."

Like the glimmer of seduction she'd spotted in his eyes, the tone of his voice held a suggestion she wasn't inclined to accept.

"Go," Porthos said, suddenly sticking his round, goateed face in front of hers, then turning to glance at Christian.

The white plume on Porthos's wide-brimmed

hat swept across her face, and Brianne sputtered as the feathers brushed across her lips.

"You and the Frenchman would make quite a handsome couple, my dear," D'Artagnan said, stroking his goatee as he moved to stand beside her.

She threw him a withering look.

"Ah, but take care not to break the poor man's heart," Aramis implored, dramatically placing both hands over his own heart and screwing his face into a mournful frown.

She glanced past them and toward Athos for help, but the tall, square-faced, and bewhiskered blond merely lazed against the entry's doorjamb, looking sullen, as he always did when anything even remotely connected to love came up.

She batted a hand at Porthos's plume, still dancing in front of her face. "Will you all please just mind your own—" Brianne stopped abruptly, clamping her mouth closed as her gaze met Christian Deuvelle's.

For fifty weeks a year she talked freely with them, not having to bother to worry if anyone was listening or watching. But it was so hard to remember that she couldn't do that during the two weeks every year that Felix opened the house to tourists.

Christian stared at her with a look that was either mild puzzlement or amusement. She wasn't sure which, but neither was good. LeiMonte Castle might have the reputation of being haunted, but since she and Felix were the only ones who could see their "roommates," that reputation didn't mean LeiMonte's guests, as well as the good people of Bayou de Joie, Louisiana, wouldn't think she was certifiably crazy if they saw her talking to thin air.

And now that she was assuming control over the company, she couldn't afford for anyone to think she was loony. That would certainly not be the way to establish herself and win respect at the executive meetings.

Brianne slipped her arm around Christian's. Better to accompany him through the gardens now, while the sun was still shining, than find herself put on the spot later, when moonlight and darkness as well as her matchmaking "roomies" might lend the stroll a more romantic ambience than she cared for. "Let me show you the Anne of Austria roses," she said cheerfully. "Uncle Felix had the original cuttings brought over from France."

The four Musketeers quickly gathered at her heels to follow.

Sensing them behind her, Brianne paused and looked back, presumably at Felix, who'd already opened his book and turned his attention to its finely printed pages. "I'll meet you back here in a little while," she said, her gaze furtively moving from one Musketeer to another.

"If you insist on doing this, milady, you need a chaperon," Athos said stolidly.

"Oh, hogwash," Porthos quipped. "Brianne's

right. How can romance blossom if we're all watching?"

"We don't *all* need to chaperon," Aramis said. "I'll go."

Porthos laughed. "Great, a chaperon who wouldn't know love if it slapped him across the face."

Aramis stiffened. "I beg your pardon. I'll have you know I enjoyed the pleasures of a great many more of the ladies of Paris than would even have given you the time of day."

"Precisely my point," Porthos said. "You enjoyed them, but you never loved any of them."

"You were a lothario," Felix mumbled.

Aramis turned to glare at the old man. "I most certainly was not!"

Brianne wished, for the millionth time, that the men in her life could get along, just once in a while. But the Musketeers had never forgiven Felix for uprooting their precious LeiMonte and transporting it, as well as them, halfway around the world. And Felix had never forgiven them for coming along. Even though they'd obviously had no choice in the matter.

"I'll meet you *all* back here in a little while," Brianne said again.

Christian placed a hand over the one she'd laid on his arm. "I really find it quite novel the way you Southerners say 'you all,' all the time."

Brianne smiled at him, then glanced back at the

other men, one red-gold brow raised as she looked at each in turn to make certain they understood.

"As you wish, milady," all four said in unison, sweeping plumed hats from their heads and bowing deeply.

Brianne smiled, though she wasn't certain she could trust them. Sometimes they were so infuriating, she wanted to scream and find a priest to exorcise them and fling them into the heavens. But other times their gallantry, their almost irresistible charm, their warmth and caring, and the stories they told of their escapades and the people they'd known, convinced her she was very lucky to have them in her life.

She walked beside Christian through the foyer and into the parlor. Its French doors, which led out to a raised terrace and the formal gardens beyond, stood open.

"Brianne?"

She paused at hearing the housekeeper call her name and walked back into the parlor.

"Oh, there you are," Mrs. Peel said, wringing her hands on her apron. "I just don't know what to do. That banging knocker caused my soufflé to fall, and I've had to start something else for dinner, and well, *they're* in the kitchen, buzzing around and moving things and—"

"Calm down, Mrs. Peel," Brianne said. "I'll take care of *them*, and then you can tell me what I can do to help you get dinner."

"Oh, you're such a lamb."

The two women turned toward the kitchen.

"But our walk," Christian called after her, obviously disappointed.

Brianne stopped and looked back at him, having totally forgotten he was there.

His brown eyes were almost depthless, his hair the color of rich earth, and his features so classically shaped, a person could swear they'd been sculpted by Michelangelo. It wasn't hard for her to see why some women would do almost anything to win Christian Deuvelle's attention.

But he didn't interest her. She quickly shook the thought aside. "Perhaps we can take it another time," she said.

He grabbed her hand, smothering it between both of his own. "I'll only let you leave me," he said, his tone huskier, softer, his French accent instilling each word with a seductive caress, "if you promise to walk with me this evening after dinner."

Brianne nearly groaned aloud. A moonlight walk. Just what she'd been trying to avoid. He was handsome, sophisticated, talented, charming, and obviously interested in her. Everything she'd thought she wanted in a man. Assuming, of course, that she wanted a man in her life, which she didn't. Running St. John Shipping since Felix's retirement had proved to be a daunting task, but she loved it, even if it left her little time for anything else—like a personal life. Trying to stay on top of things at the office while helping Felix with the Pilgrimage festivities and the guests at LeiMonte was going to put her far enough behind as it was. She didn't need the added problem of a budding relationship, even with someone as charming and handsome as Christian Deuvelle.

On the other hand, she had been feeling a bit lonely lately. It wasn't as if she *had* to work fourteen-hour days as well as weekends. And there wasn't one logical reason why she shouldn't be attracted to him. So why wasn't she falling all over herself to accept his attentions? Why wasn't her heart hammering and her pulse racing?

Mace looked at himself in the mirror in his room before going downstairs for dinner. He'd thought about wandering the grounds to get a feel for the place, but had nixed the idea. He could see the grounds very well from this closet of a room they'd stuck him in. And as for the castle, or château, or house, or whatever they wanted to call this three-story monstrosity with its varied rooflines, arched windows, turrets, and protruding balconies, if Melanstrup had his way, and Mace clearly intended to see that he did, LeiMonte Castle and its manicured grounds wouldn't be there much longer anyway, so why bother looking them over?

Anxiety hummed through his veins at the prospect of closing the deal. It would be the largest he'd ever handled.

Mace inspected himself in the mirror with a critical eye. He had no idea what the St. Johns wore for dinner or expected of their guests. The brochure had said semiformal, but in this place he wasn't sure what semiformal meant. Mardi Gras costume? Crowns, jewels, and capes? A suit? A tuxedo? He'd opted for the suit.

He grabbed the door handle and turned it.

Nothing happened.

He turned the key beneath the knob to confirm that the door was unlocked, then tried again.

Nothing.

Frowning, Mace wiped his hand on one of the guest towels that had been left on his bureau. The door and fixtures looked ancient, so obviously the blasted thing was stuck. Probably swollen from the day's heat and humidity. He grabbed the knob, held tight, and tried to twist it.

Nothing.

A flood of curses spewed from his mouth as he looked around the room. He was stuck in the damned tower. Walking to one of the windows, he threw it open and looked down. No balcony, no stairs, and he was in no shape or mood to play Rapunzel. Mace grabbed the windowsill and leaned out. He was three stories up. Shadows had crept over the landscape, invading everything, and there wasn't a soul in sight. He turned, paced the room, then went back to the window. He could yell, but somehow he found the prospect of Brianne St. John running up the stairs to rescue him from a stuck door a little too humiliating.

Moving back to the door, he grabbed its knob

with both hands, braced a foot against the wall, and pushed against it while twisting and pulling the knob at the same time.

Nothing.

"I think I'll make certain I'm here for the demolition of this place," he grumbled, "and have them aim the crushing ball at this room first."

He grabbed the doorknob and tried again.

The door sprang open, and Mace flew across the room, landing with a thud on his rear end.

"I think that worked very well, don't you?" Aramis observed, looking at Porthos.

A horribly devilish grin creased the taller Musketeer's face. "I think we let go too soon."

FOUR

Felix excused himself from the table and headed for his study.

"So, shall we take that walk you promised me, Miss St. John?" Christian asked, laying his napkin down beside his dinner plate and rising from the table. He smiled and offered a hand to Brianne.

Mace looked from their hostess to the Frenchman. This Deuvelle fellow was definitely pompous. Mace didn't know why he cared, but it appeared that each of the three women seated at the table, including Brianne St. John, not only enjoyed the man's inane witticisms, but had practically drooled over him all during their meal.

"Yes, our walk." Brianne smiled. She had hoped he'd forgotten about it.

Mace watched as Brianne placed her hand in Christian Deuvelle's and rose from her seat. A feeling of annoyance gnawed at him, but he pushed it aside. He was at LeiMonte for business, not pleasure. What did he care if Brianne St. John strolled through moonlit gardens with some affected and pretentious Frenchman?

Except, he suddenly decided, a little ticked that the old man had excused himself before Mace could suggest they talk over an after-dinner drink, Deuvelle's attentions to Felix's grandniece might interfere with Mace's plans. Perhaps he should try to ingratiate himself with her after all. If he could, it might help him figure out a way to get what Melanstrup wanted from the St. Johns. And wasn't that why Mace was there, in an antiquated, barely livable land of gators, swamps, and unbearable humidity?

He tossed his napkin down and rose. His initial investigations had not led to any logical approach to Felix St. John. The old man was a wily businessman and had always played things extremely close to the vest, both personally and professionally, which meant that if Mace used conventional means, it would take him that much longer to accomplish his goal.

From what he'd seen so far, Brianne St. John's company might prove not only valuable but pleasurable, and a definite alternative to trying to outsmart Felix St. John. It wouldn't be the first time Mace had obtained someone's help without their even being aware that they were giving it.

The decision was instant. "You know, a walk in

the garden and a little fresh air does sound like a great idea," he said.

Christian turned to stare at him, obviously dumbfounded and not at all happy at Mace's announcement.

Brianne, to Mace's delight, smiled, though whether she was actually pleased at the thought of his accompanying her and Christian into the garden, or merely being polite, he wasn't sure. Time would tell.

"Brianne," Felix said from the doorway, "have you seen my reading glasses?"

Mace's wineglass, still half-full, suddenly toppled over, the dark red liquid spreading across the highly polished table.

"Sorry," Mace mumbled, and used his napkin to stop the wine from spilling onto the floor.

Brianne looked about quickly, but other than catching the sound of a faint chuckle, she detected no Musketeer in the room. Nevertheless, she knew at least one of them was present. That wineglass hadn't overturned itself. There hadn't been anyone near it. She glanced toward Felix, who was looking at Mace Calder.

"Good reflexes," Felix said, looking around the room. "Do you fence?"

Mrs. Peel hurried forth to catch the spill.

Mace stared at the old man. "Fence?"

"My uncle used to be quite adept at the sport," Brianne interjected quickly, glaring at Felix as he nodded at her and turned to leave, a mischievous twinkle in his eyes.

"Well, shall we go?" Christian said, breaking the silence and throwing Mace a look that clearly said he wasn't wanted.

Mace smiled and motioned toward the open French doors across the room. "After you," he said, almost laughing at the Frenchman's glower.

Christian held Brianne's arm snugly within his crooked one and turned them toward the doors that led out onto the veranda and gardens.

Mace took a step to follow.

The empty chair next to the one he'd just vacated suddenly fell in front of him, its ornately carved wooden back slamming down on his foot.

"Son of a . . ."

Brianne whirled at the sound of the crash and the angry curse.

One of the other female guests stood and fluttered a hand in front of her face. "My, you know, getting some fresh air suddenly sounds like a wonderful idea." She hurried to Mace's side and slipped her arm around his. "And you," she said, "seem like you just might need a little help avoiding accidents."

Mace looked down at her. Manners dictated he be a gentleman, something he normally didn't bother with when it involved business. In fact, in the kind of business he was in, being a gentleman could be a real drawback. "Shark" was the word people usually used in reference to him. It was most often meant as an insult, but Mace had always accepted it as a compliment.

This situation, however, was different from any he'd encountered before. He was there on business, but everyone thought he was there on vacation. Subterfuge. It was not something he'd done before, and he couldn't say he was enjoying it. But he'd agreed with Melanstrup that in this case it was necessary, which meant he would have to improvise and do a few things a bit differently than usual.

He smiled at Lizbeth Raines. She was so short and petite, she seemed nearly a midget next to his six-foot-three frame.

Lizbeth gazed up at him flirtatiously, batting heavily mascaraed lashes, spreading hot-pink-painted lips into a wide smile, and flipping her long blonde hair over her shoulder with her free hand.

Several gold bracelets jangled on her wrist with the movement.

Mace felt Brianne's gaze on him. If he wanted to make a good impression on her, he needed to be gracious to her and her guests. At least for now. Perhaps he could use Lizbeth's obvious interest in him to his advantage.

"I find a walk in moonlit gardens is always more enjoyable with a beautiful woman on my arm," Mace said, drawing Lizbeth toward the open French doors.

Her eyes fairly sparkled back at him.

The other four guests rose and, declining the walk, turned toward the parlor.

Mace glanced at Brianne as they all walked outside, but if there was even the slightest hint that she was bothered by his attention to the petite blonde, he didn't see it.

"Oh, this is so beautiful," Lizbeth said as they strolled down the shell-covered path toward a white gazebo set in the center of the gardens.

Several old-fashioned torchlights lit the way, the fire within their glass globes dancing against the dark night.

Mace looked at Brianne, who had veered onto a side path and then paused beside a rosebush. She appeared deep in conversation with Christian Deuvelle. "Yes, it is," Mace murmured absently in response to Lizbeth. What did Brianne see in the man anyway? He felt another surge of the annoyance he'd experienced toward Deuvelle earlier that evening. Did she actually like him, or was she merely playing the cordial hostess?

He remembered something his secretary had said to him when he'd asked her why the background file on Brianne St. John was so thin.

She dedicated herself to her schooling, her uncle, and that castle, while she was growing up. Didn't date a lot, never had much of a social life away from Felix St. John, and she still doesn't.

Mace watched the way the moonlight played in the long strands of Brianne's hair, turning them to cascading waves of gold-touched flame.

Lizbeth Raines said something he didn't catch,

so Mace merely nodded, hoping it would suffice for an answer.

He could almost feel his fingers slipping slowly through those red-gold tangles, and knew it would not be difficult to mix pleasure with business during this trip if Brianne St. John was the pleasure.

"Miss Raines?"

Mace and Lizbeth paused and looked back.

Mrs. Peel was standing on the veranda. "You have a phone call. A Mr. Lovelle."

Lizbeth gasped. "Harlen?" She pulled her arm from Mace's. "Oh, please excuse me, I must take that. I'll meet you in the reception hall in the morning."

Mace stared at her blankly.

"Say, eightish?"

He nodded, wondering what he had agreed to. Hopefully it was nothing more than breakfast. Before he could figure a way to ask her, however, she hurried toward the house.

Mace turned back to Christian and Brianne, who had walked farther away from him into the garden. He followed, his stride purposeful. If he was going to make any headway with Brianne St. John, now was as good a time to start as any.

"So, Miss St. John, tell me about this annual Barataria Pilgrimage," Mace said, moving to stand close to her. "What kind of activities can I expect to encounter?"

"How about trying out the beheading block?" D'Artagnan suggested. "Or the guillotine?"

Brianne stifled the groan that instantly rose to her lips at the sight of the Musketeer. She looked at Mace and forced herself to smile.

Mace detected an uneasiness in her, but whether it was due to his presence or Deuvelle's, he wasn't sure.

"Well, let me think," Brianne said.

"Perhaps he'd prefer a duel?" Porthos offered, drawing his sword. "To which I would be most happy to oblige."

He swished the long blade about, and Brianne felt a soft swirl of air brush her arm. She turned abruptly, as if she'd heard something in the bushes beyond where they stood, and glared a warning at the two Musketeers, though she knew from experience that they would blissfully ignore it.

"I think he's English," D'Artagnan said, as if that was explanation enough for their comments and dislike of Mace.

Brianne raised her brows in question.

"We don't trust him."

Terrific. She turned back to Mace and Christian with a smile plastered on her face but anger burning in her breast. In the past two years she'd had all of three dates. Everything had gone fine with each of them, until the men had brought her home. That's when the gates of hell had opened up on them in the form of four meddling but well-meaning Musketeers. None of her dates had ever called again.

If she ever seriously decided to look for a husband, Brianne knew she'd be in trouble, because her "roomies" didn't seem to share her taste in men.

"Well," Brianne said finally, "there's the fair at the far end of town. And all the antebellum homes in the area will be open, as well as several that date back even further. There's also . . ."

Mace knew she was still talking, but he wasn't really interested in the sights of the small Louisiana town, and so he let his mind wander. Her perfume seemed to surround him, the scent distinctly different from the cloying fragrance of the garden flowers. The redolence that emanated from Brianne teased his senses and reminded him of cool spring days and the wildflowers that had grown in the open fields he'd played in as a kid.

"There are plenty of brochures regarding the local festivities on the table in the reception hall," Christian said. His tone was frigid as he cut Brianne off and made no effort to hide the glower he directed at Mace.

"Really?" Mace laughed. "Guess I missed them. But"—he looked at Brianne—"I find it's almost always better to get a personal recommendation, don't you?"

She nodded. She'd delivered this discourse on tourist sights so many times, she could do it without thinking, so her thoughts had been elsewhere. Specifically on the two Musketeers who, only she was aware, were standing nearby. They'd become too silent, and that made her nervous.

"Perhaps we should return to the house," Christian said. "It's late and I'm sure everyone would like to relax in the parlor over a sherry before retiring."

Mace saw his opportunity and seized it. "Why don't you go on ahead, Deuvelle, since you're tired." He took Brianne's hand. "I have a few more questions I'd like to ask our hostess, so I'll walk Miss St. John back in a minute." He looked at Brianne. "If she doesn't mind?"

Brianne had a hunch doing anything with Mace Calder would be asking for trouble, but D'Artagnan and Porthos remained silent. Mace's dark eyes held hers and for a few seconds she forgot her hesitations. Then Porthos cleared his throat and the sound snapped Brianne back to reality. "Thank you, Mr. Calder, but I have had a long day, and I am tired. I think I'd just better—"

"Just a few minutes," Mace cajoled, "I promise."

A few minutes. She glanced at Porthos and D'Artagnan. How much damage could they do in a few minutes?

Plenty, a small voice in the back of her mind whispered.

The two Musketeers smiled at her, and that made Brianne even more apprehensive.

"I don't think Miss St. John wants to stay out here any longer," Christian snapped, taking Brianne's free hand and possessively tucking it within the crook of his arm. "It's getting late."

"Good move," D'Artagnan said.

Great. Brianne looked from one man to the next. First D'Artagnan and Porthos, and then Deuvelle and Mace Calder. Were there any men on the planet, dead or alive, who were not argumentative and troublesome? "Mr. Deuvelle," she said, pulling her hand free and trying not to sound too exasperated, "thank you, but I'm fine. I'll stay and answer Mr. Calder's questions and see you in the morning."

She was tempting fate and would probably end up the loser, but she didn't like being dictated to, by the living or the dead!

Mace looked at Christian and smiled.

The Frenchman realized he'd been outmaneuvered and turned to Brianne. Taking her free hand again, he bent and pressed his lips to her knuckles. "Until tomorrow, *chérie*," he said softly. "Dream of me."

Mace felt like gagging, then like punching the man's lights out. Dream of me. Hah! The prospect of anyone dreaming about Christian Deuvelle impressed him as more of a nightmare.

Brianne watched Christian walk away. She had a sneaky feeling the man didn't take rejection well, which meant she'd have to be very careful with him. The last thing she needed was anyone bad-mouthing LeiMonte Castle. Felix would turn purple, and that wouldn't be good for either his heart or his blood pressure. She turned to Mace. "So, Mr. Calder, what questions did you have for me?"

"Call me Mace."

"Mace," Porthos said with a growl. He jerked two ugly, spiked metal balls from his belt and began spinning them from their connecting chain. "*This* is a mace!"

Brianne struggled to ignore Porthos and simultaneously prayed he wouldn't be able to exert the extra burst of plasmic energy that would enable him to wrap his weapon about Mace Calder's neck. That type of materialization each of the Musketeers could only do on special occasions—their birthdays, the date of their deaths, anniversaries.

As Porthos scowled Brianne felt assured this wasn't "one of his days" and in relief turned her attention back to Mace. "That's not a question," she said. Her gaze moved over his face. A sense of uneasiness invaded her as she experienced the feeling that she'd seen Mace Calder before, but she couldn't remember where. Though the feeling and the idea itself were innocent enough, she had the distinct impression that innocence was about as far away from Mace Calder as the devil was from heaven.

FIVE

"I understand your uncle recently retired and left you in charge of St. John Shipping," Mace said.

"Yes." Brianne looked at him curiously. She had expected him to ask questions about the castle or the festival.

"You don't look the type to be running a multi-million-dollar company."

"Oh, and what type is that, Mr. Calder?" Brianne said, instantly indignant. She was very much aware that there were many people, mostly men, and mostly all employed at St. John Shipping, who didn't believe her capable of running the company. "Male?"

He smiled, and though she'd just been more than a bit put off by his comment, she found herself unreasonably admiring the way his strong features softened slightly with the upward curve of his lips.

"Touché," Mace said.

"Touché," Porthos mocked. "The man probably doesn't even know the meaning of the word." He drew a pair of well-sharpened knives he kept sheathed on either side of his belt. Holding both in one hand, handles crossed, he sliced the air with them and jumped in front of Mace, still swinging the deadly mace in his other hand. *"En garde,"* he yelled, glaring.

Mace paused.

Brianne held her breath.

Taking a step forward, Mace walked right through the tall Musketeer.

Brianne nearly sagged in relief.

"Damn the stars," Porthos spat, tossing the mace and watching it zip through Mace Calder and continue on its way until it had disappeared from sight.

Brianne bit down on her bottom lip to keep from laughing.

Glowering at her, Porthos spun on his heel and stalked away, disappearing before he'd taken more than a few steps.

Brianne looked about for D'Artagnan, then decided he'd either purposely made himself invisible to her, or he'd left too.

D'Artagnan knelt down in front of Serendipity.

The large cat, asleep on one of the parlor chairs, opened an eye lazily.

"Listen, beautiful," the Musketeer said softly, "you need to go out into the garden and"—he glanced back over his shoulder to make certain neither Felix nor Brianne was around—"make awful with that Englishman. Scratch him or something."

Serendipity closed her eye and snuggled her head deeper into the cradle of her arm.

"Dippy!" D'Artagnan snapped.

The cat's eye opened. She stood, stretched, jumped from the chair, and pranced into the foyer.

"Not *that* way," D'Artagnan yelled, watching as the huge white cat bounded up the grand staircase.

"So, you only open your home to guests during the festival?" Mace said, drawing Brianne's attention.

She nodded as they turned off the garden's main walkway onto a smaller one. "Yes."

"And it really was brought over stone by stone from France?"

"My uncle wanted the real thing. He was traveling through France, and when he saw LeiMonte he fell in love with it. Of course, its colorful history helped."

"Wait, I remember what I read in the brochure," Mace said, and chuckled. "The meeting place of the famous four Musketeers. I always thought they were a product of Alexandre Dumas's imagination."

Brianne shook her head. "No, they are . . .

were," she corrected quickly, "very much real. LeiMonte belonged to Athos and was used by himself and his wife, Charlotte, as a summer retreat when he was the Comte de la Fère."

Mace frowned. "But didn't that little history section of your brochure mention something about her betraying him and each thinking the other dead, and then him finally arresting her?"

"Yes. It's a long story and not a happy one. In the end she was charged with treason and executed."

"Oh, great guy."

Brianne looked at him sharply, then hoped Athos was nowhere within hearing distance. "There's much more to the story than that, Mr. Calder, but let's just end it by saying that he truly loved her and she forgave him at the end."

"Magnanimous, to say the least."

"She loved him."

"And ended up dead as a result."

"She ended up dead, Mr. Calder," Brianne snapped, "because she tried to betray France. It was just Athos's misfortune to have been the one to catch her."

"He could have let her go."

Brianne sighed and shook her head. She'd thought the same thing once, but that was before she'd actually come to know the handsome blond Musketeer. "No. He was a king's Musketeer, he couldn't turn his back on his duty, and he's had to live with that sorrow ever since."

"So he grieved over her until the day he died," Mace said.

And beyond, Brianne added silently.

"Big of him," Mace continued, "for all the good it did her."

Brianne stared at him, anger pounding in her temples. He obviously didn't have a compassionate bone in his body. But then, in her experience, most men didn't.

As if sensing her mood, Mace plucked a rose from its stem, turned, and smiled at her. If he was going to get on her good side, he wasn't going about it in the best way. "For milady," he said, offering her the rose and bowing gallantly. "Forgive me."

Brianne suddenly found her anger melting away.

As they resumed their stroll, she related the unconfirmed legend that four of the building's stones actually contained the caskets of the Musketeers.

"Really? Encased in stone?" Mace said, feigning interest. He was starting to find that the old tale, as well as his reason for being at LeiMonte Castle, was the furthest thing from his mind.

"So the legend goes."

A devilish smile played on Mace's features. "But if the ghosts are here, as you say, why don't you just ask them?"

The gleam of mischief she saw in his eyes was contagious. "Maybe I have."

Mace laughed and casually guided Brianne

Never Alone

down one of the garden's meandering, rosebush-lined paths. He had intended to question her about Felix St. John and her involvement with the company. Her answers could provide the information he needed if he was to accomplish his goal, but listening to her talk about the castle, watching the way the moonlight played off her features and danced within the reddish-gold strands of her hair had taken his thoughts in another direction, and it was one he was unreasonably unwilling to change at the moment.

An almost full moon lay cradled within the star-specked darkness of the sky, its vibrant rays caressing the landscape.

At a small clearing Brianne paused to pick several roses to take back to the house.

Mace watched, surprised by the desire he felt to pull her into his arms and kiss her.

"Don't even think about it, *mon ami*," Aramis whispered as he appeared beside Mace.

Mace rolled his shoulders against the sudden chill of cold air that seemed to surround him, and his dark brows pulled together in a frown of puzzlement. He looked around. Unless he was going crazy, he'd swear he had just heard someone say something, yet the words had been too soft to decipher, and Brianne was too far away to have spoken them.

"There, I think these will look nice on the drawing-room table, don't you?" Brianne said, holding up the bouquet she'd picked. She stopped when she saw Aramis. "What are you doing here?"

Mace frowned. "What? Waiting for you."

The handsomest of the Musketeers bowed deeply. "Looking out for you, milady," he said. He smiled wickedly, blue eyes twinkling with mischief, his aristocratic features touched with just the right amount of concern. Not for the first time Brianne found herself marveling that there had been even one woman left in France who had not fallen prey to the charms of this devastatingly attractive Musketeer.

Brianne glanced from Aramis to Mace, suddenly realizing she'd spoken aloud. "Oh, I'm sorry, Mr. Calder. I was thinking of something else for a moment." She raised a rose to her nose as if to sniff its fragrance and, with her lips hidden from Mace's view, whispered hurriedly, "Don't make trouble."

Aramis's dark brows went up. "Me? Make trouble?" He slapped a hand over his heart. "Oh, milady, you wound me."

"I wish I could."

"Pardon?" Mace said.

"Oh, I said this rose smells wonderful."

Mace watched her approach and wondered what it was about her that had him forgetting business and thinking about pleasure. That was unusual for him.

She paused before him and carefully broke off part of the flower's stem. "Here." She reached up

Never Alone

and slipped the blossom into the buttonhole of his lapel.

Aramis appeared at her side. "You've never given me a rose."

She threw Aramis a look that clearly said "later."

Mace looked down at the white flower whose petals had half closed for the night, then back up at her. He took the rose from where she'd placed it and slipped it within the strands of her hair. "I think it looks much lovelier here," he said.

"And you're going to look lovelier six feet under," Aramis said with a growl.

Brianne blushed and tried to ignore Aramis's scowling presence, as well as the heat that was suddenly coursing through her veins.

Mace found himself mesmerized. "Go to the festival with me tomorrow," he said impulsively. "Show me the real Bayou de Joie."

"The real Bayou de Joie," Brianne echoed. She smiled mischievously. "You mean—"

"Yes, show him the real Bayou de Joie by Barataria Bay," Aramis interrupted. "And if Lafitte is any kind of Frenchman at all, he'll show up and lend a hand"—he chuckled—"or a sword, in giving our friend here a real treat."

"He's dead."

"Who's dead?" Mace asked.

"Well, so am I, milady, *n'est-ce pas?*" Aramis crowed, and bowed gracefully. "But I am here nevertheless."

"Unfortunately."

Aramis mockingly clutched at his heart and looked heavenward. "Ah, you wound me again."

"Unfortunately what?" Mace echoed, becoming more confused each time she spoke.

Brianne fumed. This was leading toward nothing but trouble, and she didn't have time for it. She had work to do. She turned back to Mace and smiled. "I'm sorry, Mr. Calder. I was just thinking of something I need to take care of and, ah, sometimes I mumble aloud. Now, if you really feel the need of a guide for the festival, I can recommend several very good ones."

He looked down at her for a long moment, wondering if he needed his hearing checked or if Brianne St. John was as loony as her uncle's precious castle was haunted.

"Call me Mace," he said, deciding instantly to ignore her decidedly offbeat conversation. He needed personal information about Felix St. John, and where better to get it than from his niece? "And I'd rather you be my guide."

"Ah, and what else?" Aramis whispered over her shoulder.

Brianne whirled to face him. "Go away!"

Mace stared at her back. "Excuse me?"

"He's not right for you, *ma petite*," Aramis said. "He's not . . ."

Brianne glared at him. "French?"

The Musketeer's handsome face broke into a smug smile and he crossed his arms. "Exactly."

Never Alone

"Go away."

A glower instantly replaced the smile. "Oh, all right, but don't say I didn't warn you." With that, Aramis spun on his heel, sending his blue-and-silver cloak swirling about him, and disappeared into the settling shadows of night.

Mace purposely cleared his throat to get her attention.

She turned back to him. "Oh, sorry." Think, Brianne, think, she ordered herself as her mind spun for some explanation she could offer for talking to someone he couldn't see. "There's, ah, an old Cajun superstition in the bayou. Um, whenever you see a crack of lightning or hear a roll of distant thunder, it means a summer storm is coming in. If you don't want it to rain, you face the threat and command it to go away and it will."

It sounded stupid even to her own ears.

Mace's brows quirked in disbelief.

Brianne laughed. "Well, it doesn't hurt to be just a little bit superstitious, Mr. Calder. You never know what might work, and it would be a shame for the festival to be ruined by rain."

"I didn't hear or see anything."

"Really?" Brianne shrugged. "Maybe you just weren't paying attention, Mr. Calder."

"Mace."

She nodded. "Mace."

"You didn't answer my question about the festival. Will you go with me?"

"And show you the *real* Bayou de Joie?" Brianne said. "Like the pirate Lafitte's hideout, the tavern where he and his men sat, drank, and planned their next raid, and maybe even where he supposedly hid his treasure?"

Mace shrugged. "That, and perhaps where an eager Californian can take a Southern lady to lunch and get to know her a little better."

Something about the way he looked at her, the curve of one corner of his mouth, or the way one dark brow rose ever so slightly, sent an uncomfortable flash of déjà vu sweeping through Brianne's body.

"What kind of business are you in, exactly?" she asked, suddenly wanting to know more about this man who was causing a myriad of conflicting emotions to speed through her body.

"Investments," he said. "And you're avoiding the subject of being my guide."

"I have other guests to see to. And work to do."

Mace reached out and touched her hand, brushing his fingers lightly down its side.

Brianne shivered and looked up at him, but she didn't pull away.

Desire warmed Mace's blood. He had come to LeiMonte Castle for one reason and one reason only, but all that was forgotten now, because all he wanted to do was kiss her.

Brianne looked into his eyes and knew what he was thinking, what he wanted to do. Their gazes fused, and though each knew, for their own reasons, that it would be better to step back, to move away from this encounter, to stop things before they went any further, neither acted on the knowledge.

The scent of a subtle yet exotic spice blended with that of virile male and filled her senses like an ancient aphrodisiac, while the feel of his fingertips skimming lightly over her hand sent fire through her blood. She saw his lips part, his head begin to lower toward hers.

There was no room for a love relationship in her life. It would not, could not work. She owed Felix too much, could never leave him, could never leave the company.

Yet, unlike other times, with other men, at this moment that argument wasn't working. The attraction she'd been feeling toward Mace Calder was no longer deniable. Neither was her desire to feel his lips upon hers.

She felt his hand move lightly up the length of her arm, felt his fingers, warm and strong, settle around her flesh. His breath danced over her cheek as he neared, a soul-touching caress that left her aching for more.

He was going to kiss her. She knew she should stop him, knew she should pull away from this man who was a stranger to her. The Musketeers had obviously already taken a thorough dislike to him. That could only mean trouble. She had work to do, obligations to fulfill.

She remained still.

His lips were like a touch of fire to hers. Passion, hot and overwhelming, coursed through Brianne like flames sweeping across a dry prairie, drawing need and hunger along with it, engulfing every fiber and nerve in her body, routing all rational considerations, and leaving her only thought that of him.

The bouquet of roses slipped from her hands and fell to the ground as she swayed against him, her body pressing to his as if, without his support, she would melt into the earth.

Mace slipped his arms around her waist and pulled her close.

Brianne slid her arms over his shoulders and wrapped them around his neck, clinging to him as the heady scents of the bayou clung to the night. His tongue, like a hot serpent of desire, stroked hers, and she reveled in the passion each silken caress fueled within her body. She moaned softly, the sound traveling no farther from her throat than to his. This was a moment she wanted never to end, a kiss she prayed would go on forever.

Her body burned hot with a need she had never felt before.

"Bon Dieu," Aramis snapped. "I don't believe this. I leave you alone with this . . . this rogue for only a few moments and—"

Startled, Brianne jerked away from Mace and spun to face Aramis.

"—things go *de mal en pis*! From bad to worse!"

She looked back at Mace. What had she been thinking?

That's the problem, her own conscience whispered to her, *you* weren't *thinking*.

Fear, anger, and contrition seized her. "That . . . that was a mistake, Mr. Calder." She bent and hurriedly scooped up the fallen roses with trembling hands. "I'm sorry. I . . . I think we'd just better forget it even happened." Brianne rose and, without looking at him, brushed past Mace and hurried toward the house.

Mace stared after her. A mistake? He struggled against the fire of passion still swirling through his blood as anger swept through his thoughts. A mistake? Anger turned to fury. That was supposed to be his line when it came time to leave here . . . not hers!

He fumed. The last thing he needed in his life was any kind of romantic entanglement. He'd had enough of that kind of thing to give him a headful of bad memories. All he wanted was to get some information about Brianne St. John's uncle. That's it. He didn't care about her.

So why in the hell did it bother him that she'd just brushed him off like so much dander on an old jacket?

SIX

Brianne hurried through the foyer and dumped her bouquet of roses on the kitchen counter.

"Mercy, child, whatever is the matter with you?" Mrs. Peel said, turning from the slab of pie crust she was busily rolling out on the table. "You look white as a sheet."

"I . . . I have a headache."

Serendipity wove her generously-sized body in and out of Brianne's ankles.

"Well land sakes, honey, take some aspirin. I saw you go into the garden with that Mr. Deuvelle earlier, so it's no wonder you have a headache." Mrs. Peel threw flour onto the dough and continued to move her rolling pin over it without pause. "That man's enough to drive a person to murder; flitting around like a crazed bird half the time, asking questions and waving his arms about, and skulking in the shadows the other half of the time.

He near scared me to death this morning, popping out of that little alcove in the hall upstairs. Thought my heart was gonna stop right then and there."

"You've been reading your vampire books again, haven't you?" Brianne teased.

"Wouldn't be surprised if that was exactly what the man was," she said, flipping her dough. "Pretty as sin on the outside, but inside . . ." She shook her head.

Brianne smiled. Mrs. Peel always had a unique way of describing their guests. She wondered what opinion the older woman held of Mace Calder. The mere thought of him brought back a swirl of feelings and turned her legs to rubber. "Could you put those flowers in the vase with the others in the drawing room, Mrs. Peel? I think I'll call it an early evening and go upstairs." She started for the door to the foyer.

"Take the servants' stairs, honey," Mrs. Peel said as she turned toward the sink. "Otherwise that loony Frenchman Deuvelle just might nab you. Last I saw, he was still in the parlor examining each piece of furniture as if it were some long-lost piece of treasure stolen from his ancestors' house or something." She shook her head. "Crazy man."

Brianne turned toward a small archway in the outer corner of the room. "Thanks," she mumbled, and hurried up the narrow spiral staircase.

She paused at the top of the stairs, peeked out into the wide second-floor hallway to make certain no one was about, then dashed toward her bedroom door. Once inside the room, she breathed a sigh of relief, grabbed her nightgown, and hurriedly undressed.

Christian dropped to his knees and ran a hand along the bottom of the old wing chair.

"No bulges or seams where there shouldn't be any. It's probably been reupholstered several times anyway," he mumbled to himself. "And who knows where it even really came from." He rose.

His task would have been simpler if he'd had a way of verifying which, if any, of the pieces of furniture at LeiMonte were original to the place. But since that wasn't possible, he merely had to check them all, along with the walls, cornices, bookshelves, and every other nook and cranny he could find. There was no telling where it could be hidden.

A soft curse of frustration slipped from his lips as he looked back at the chair he'd just examined. It was the last piece in the parlor. His gaze moved slowly about the room. There had proven to be no hidden panels around the windows or doors, and so far he'd found none within the paneled walls. There was nothing of note around the marble face of the fireplace, the bricks inside its grate, or the bookshelves that lined one wall. He looked up at the ornate molding that edged the ceiling. It was impossible to check, but he doubted what he was looking for was there anyway. He couldn't quite see Lady de Winter climbing up so high.

Somewhere else in the house a door closed.

Christian hurriedly sat down and grabbed the book he'd brought into the parlor in case anyone interrupted him. He flipped it open and stared unseeingly at the page.

A second later the house fell back into silence.

Christian set the book aside and rose, turning toward the fireplace. Maybe in its ornately carved mantel somewhere . . .

Brianne smiled as Serendipity jumped onto her bed. "So, what kind of trouble have you been getting into today, my beauty?"

The huge white cat walked in a circle several times, kneaded the thick bedspread for a few seconds, then settled down and turned her green eyes on Brianne. A soft purr rumbled from her body.

"Not telling, huh?" Brianne laughed and slid under the covers, then reached out a hand and stroked the cat's large body. "About time you should be having these kittens, don't you think?"

Serendipity laid her head down and closed her eyes.

Brianne smiled and snuggled beneath the covers, letting her body relax into the goose-down mattress and mound of pillows propped against her headboard.

An image of Mace Calder's face instantly

floated through her mind. The blood in her veins warmed. Her heartbeat accelerated. Brianne's eyes popped open and she sat up, slapping a hand down on the bed.

Serendipity's eyes opened and she looked at Brianne in annoyance.

"I know I've seen that man before." She scrunched her eyes shut and rubbed at them with her fingers, as if that would help her remember. "But where?" she mumbled. "Where have I seen him?"

"On a wanted poster perhaps?" Aramis offered, suddenly materializing at the end of her bed, one hip and leg propped lazily on her mattress.

Brianne bolted upright and jerked the sheet to her chest. "You didn't knock!"

He smiled, but the glint she saw in his blue eyes was anything but sheepish. "Sorry, but I came through the fireplace." He hooked an arm over the bed's elaborately carved footboard. "Knocking on marble doesn't work too well, *ma petite*."

D'Artagnan walked through the closed entry door, sweeping his multiplumed hat from his head and throwing it toward a table across the room. "*Quelle audace! Quelle audace! Quelle audace et toujours quelle audace!*"

"*Aux armes?*" Aramis said, looking at D'Artagnan and grinning.

Brianne jumped at D'Artagnan's sudden appearance and outburst and stared from one Musketeer to the other, not having the faintest idea what they were saying. A little French she could understand, but when one or all of them really got going, she was lost.

D'Artagnan began to pace, cursing under his breath with each step.

Brianne's indignation returned. "Did I call a meeting in my room and then forget about it?" she asked.

Across the room D'Artagnan spun on his heel and stalked back toward her. *"De l'audace. Fils de putain. De l'audace."*

Brianne began to fume at the intrusion. "If you're going to fuss about, you could at least speak English."

"He moved my things!" D'Artagnan said again. Ramming clenched fists on his hips, he glared at her expectantly. "That son of a—"

"D'Artagnan," Brianne yelped.

"—charwoman had the audacity to move my things!"

Brianne sighed and pushed herself up to a sitting position in her bed. "What things?" she asked.

"My inkwell. Snuffbox. Parchment. Just pushed them all aside on my desk as if they were nothing and set up some little box contraption. You have to get rid of him, Brianne. He's . . . he's . . ."

"Box contraption?" Brianne said, momentarily ignoring the rest of D'Artagnan's tirade.

"Like you have in the study," he snapped, obviously exasperated. "But smaller." He positioned his hands about twelve inches apart. "Like this. Stupid thing with its lights and whistles and pictures."

"A computer?"

"Just brushed them aside as if they were nothing," he mumbled. "And that snuffbox is pure silver. Cost me a fortune, and I doubt the heathen would even have cared if it had fallen to the floor."

"Did it?" Brianne asked.

"No."

"Then there's no harm done."

"No harm done?" he sputtered. "He moved my things! *Bon Dieu*, have we no rights in our own home? What will the man do next?"

"I got him," Porthos said, jumping through the door with a flourish, brandishing his sword, and twirling around.

Brianne nearly moaned at his words. They were all too familiar, and they always meant trouble. She knew she was going to regret asking, but she had to. "Just what do you mean, you got him?"

He beamed proudly, his round, boyish face bright with delight. "I reached into that box thing of his, twirled my hand around, and the wires shorted. Thing went off just like that." He snapped his fingers. "Damned useful, this cold air we can throw out." He frowned. "Of course, it would have been better—more effective—if today was one of my days."

Brianne sent up a silent prayer of thanks that it wasn't.

"But I'll tell you, that man has a temper."

Porthos shook his head, smiled, and slashed the air with his sword. "Too bad we can't actually duel."

Brianne sent up another note of gratitude.

"I'd love to parry him a thrust or two, but it just isn't the same when they can't see you." He paused and looked at Brianne. "You know? I mean, where's the challenge in dueling with someone who doesn't even stand a sporting chance?"

She threw herself down on the bed and covered her head with a pillow. "I don't want to hear any more," she wailed, her voice muffled. "Go away."

"Do you know, *ma petite*," Aramis said rather indignantly as he rose, "that yours is the only lady's bedchamber I have ever been ordered to leave?"

Brianne looked up. "I'm honored."

"Hah! What about Lady Montague?" Porthos challenged. "I seem to remember you scrambling out of her window with your clothes in one hand and—"

"Only because that brute of a husband of hers came in," Aramis said. He smiled wickedly. "Not because the lady asked me to leave. Actually, I think she would have preferred quite the contrary."

Brianne threw the pillow aside and sat up. "Enough."

The three turned to look at her.

Her eyes suddenly narrowed as her gaze moved from one to the other. Suspicion swelled within her breast. "Where's Athos?"

"Athos?" Aramis echoed.

Porthos looked around the room.

"What is the date?" D'Artagnan suddenly asked.

Brianne glanced at the little calendar clock on her night table, then back at the Musketeer. "The fifteenth." The moment she said it, she understood the significance of his baffling question. She met D'Artagnan's gaze.

"The anniversary of his marriage to that woman."

Brianne heard the bitterness in his voice and wondered how, after all these years, he could still hold such feelings toward Athos's traitorous wife. She lay down and drew the covers up to her neck. "I know you don't need to sleep, but I do, so do you think the three of you can at least try to behave yourselves for a while?"

"Of course, milady." D'Artagnan bowed deeply, then moved to retrieve his hat.

"And stay out of the Tower Room," Brianne called after them as they disappeared through the wall.

She almost felt sorry for Mace Calder. He might not believe in ghosts, but that didn't matter, especially if the Musketeers decided to "set him straight" about a few things.

Lying back down, Brianne wondered if she should go to the Tower Room and make certain Mace Calder was all right. Instead she drew the covers over her head and snuggled deeper into her bed, her body suddenly assailed by a hot flush.

Never Alone
71

Mace stood before one of the windows of his room and looked down at the moonlit lawn that spread away from the house and disappeared within the dark shadows created by a thick copse of trees.

You don't know how to feel, Mace, how to love. You have no heart. You go from one financial conquest to another, and that's really all you care about. Business.

Stephanie Rothenberg's parting words echoed through his mind. He remembered the night she'd decided to return the engagement ring he'd bought her. He had just negotiated the takeover of Tungsten Leather that afternoon, and they'd been scheduled to have a celebratory dinner with his client, the victor. Instead, when he'd arrived to pick her up, she'd met him at the door in jeans and a sweatshirt rather than the evening gown he'd expected. He'd gotten angry and snapped at her for not being ready. She'd waited until he was done, then handed him the ring. He had forgotten it was her birthday.

It hadn't been the first special occasion he'd forgotten or let slip by, but it had been the last straw for Stephanie.

Mace heard the wireless fax on his computer beep, signaling an incoming message, but he ignored it and continued to stare out at the night-shrouded landscape. So he wasn't like other people. So what? At least he didn't fall in and out of love at the blink of an eye the way his younger brother,

Brent, did, or spend his afternoons lying on a shrink's couch like his sister, whose husband had flown the coop with his secretary.

He remembered the way he'd felt in the garden earlier with Brianne St. John, the heat and hunger that had sliced through him when he'd kissed her. Not merely the usual stirrings of desire or passion. It had been different.

Mace cursed. He didn't want different.

Suddenly a man dressed in a plumed hat and cloak moved across the lawn, but as abruptly as the figure appeared, it was gone. Mace started, blinked his eyes, and leaned closer to the window.

"What the hell?" He stared at the now-empty lawn. The man had been walking across the wide expanse of greenery, and he couldn't have moved fast enough in that second to get to the edge. Mace's gaze darted toward the dark shadows of the trees, then back toward the house. Nothing stirred.

It was as if the man had just . . . disappeared.

Mace's fax software beeped again and he turned from the window. Even with the help of the computer engineer at Melanstrup's office, whom Mace had called at home, it had taken over an hour to reprogram his computer and get it running again, and he still wasn't even certain why it had stopped in the first place. Neither was Melanstrup's engineer, and the man was one of the best.

Moving to the desk, Mace looked at the screen. He had received two faxes. One from his office in Dallas, the other from Stephanie.

He moved the cursor to the message from his office and clicked. A few weeks before he would have gone immediately to the other message. Or more likely, if he'd been in San Francisco, he would have gone directly to Stephanie's apartment and slid into bed with her.

Mace stared absently at the screen as the message from his secretary took form on the monitor.

But his thoughts continued to stray.

What would it be like to slip between the sheets with Brianne St. John? To feel her body, warm and naked next to his?

SEVEN

"*Bonjour*, everyone," Christian called merrily, practically waltzing into the dining room. "I don't think I've slept so well in ages." He passed those already seated at the table and moved to an ornately carved sideboard that sat between the east windows of the room. Lifting the lid of one steaming silver buffet tray after another, he oohed and aahed. "Oh, everything smells so delicious." He tossed his hands up and then clapped them together. "I think I actually have the appetite of a horse this morning."

"Then perhaps you should eat in the barn," Mace mumbled under his breath. He caught Brianne's glance but knew she couldn't have heard him.

She turned away and smiled at the Frenchman. "Good morning, Mr. Deuvelle."

Christian smiled over his shoulder at her. "Isn't

it, though?" He turned back to the sideboard, and the happy face disappeared as he ladled food onto his plate. His appetite was indeed healthier than normal this morning, but it had nothing to do with a good night's sleep. Rather, he was ravenous because he had physically worn himself out the previous night searching three of the downstairs rooms before giving up and finally going to bed . . . totally frustrated.

Mace glanced from Brianne to the Frenchman and felt like growling. In response to his earlier inquiry as to Felix's whereabouts, Brianne had explained that he'd gone into town to see a friend. So much for talking to Felix. That meant Mace needed to get his plan into action and zero in on Brianne. One thing he absolutely didn't need was interference from Peter Pan Deuvelle.

He looked back at Brianne, felt a stirring in his loins, shifted his weight on the chair, and silently ordered his libido to calm down. It wasn't as if she was the only attractive woman he'd seen lately. His gaze shifted to Lizbeth Raines.

Her eyes met his and she smiled.

No feelings of warmth swept through Mace's blood or stirred his desires. What in blazes was there about Brianne St. John that stirred him to thoughts of passion? He tugged at the inseam of his pants, which suddenly felt a bit snug.

Mace forced his mind back to business. The best thing he could do for himself was get the information he needed for Melanstrup's deal and get the hell away from LeiMonte, which meant he needed to work fast and pour on the charm with Brianne St. John. He smiled at her. "I thought, if you have the time after breakfast, Miss St. John, I could persuade you to show me around the place? And maybe afterward you could attend the festival with me?"

Brianne felt a flutter of sensation move through her veins, and she looked up quickly. His eyes instantly caught and held hers. Invisible shackles held her gaze prisoner, refusing to allow her to look away. Her fingers tightened around the fork she was holding as the strong sense of familiarity she'd felt when looking at Mace Calder swept over her again. "Well, I don't know. I do have some phone calls to answer, and—"

"Oh, do give him a tour of the place, Brianne," Porthos said, suddenly appearing behind Mace's chair and leaning over his shoulder to look across the table at her. He grinned widely. "I'll even go along to help." One eyebrow arched upward. "It'll be fun."

"I can wait until after you make your phone calls," Mace offered.

"Yes, we can wait," Porthos echoed.

"Oh, a private tour does sound grand," Christian said, settling at the table. He picked up his linen napkin and slapped it open with a flick of his hand, then turned and smiled a sly little smile at Brianne. "And you can tell us all the secrets of LeiMonte and its former inhabitants."

LeiMonte's other guests—the middle-aged Dr. Winston and his much younger wife, Cindy, and the Carfoiles, a snooty couple from San Francisco who looked as if they'd never seen a day of sunshine, eagerly nodded in unison.

Mace threw Christian a why-don't-you-drop-dead look, which he normally reserved for people who were threatening to ruin one of his deals.

Brianne smiled sweetly. "Well, we'll see." She looked around at everyone. "Did you all sleep well?"

Several voices began chattering at once.

"I saw a woman in my room last night," Cindy Winston said, grabbing everyone's attention. "She just floated right through the door and hovered over our bed, looking down at us."

"How much did *she* have to drink last night?" Porthos sneered.

Cindy looked at Brianne. "Are my husband and I, by any chance, sleeping in Lady de Winter's room?"

Brianne smiled. "No, I'm afraid not. That room is . . . not used." She glanced at Porthos, who was now frowning. Athos had forbade anyone from even going into his late wife's room. Felix had dared to defy him during his reconstruction and decoration of the house, and Athos had caused such a torrent of wind to break out in the room that Felix had nearly been killed. The room had been sealed ever since.

At least against mortal entry. But Brianne was

certain that every year on the anniversary of the death of Charlotte Backson, the Comtesse de la Fère, Milady de Winter, her room was where Athos retreated, to be nearer to her in his endless grief.

Everyone began talking again, questioning Cindy Winston about her supposed visitation.

Brianne slowly looked about at each person, not realizing until too late, when her gaze again swept toward Mace's, that she'd been trying to avoid looking at him. His deep blue eyes captured hers and silently, mercilessly, refused to let go. She suddenly felt herself being pulled into those infinitely dark depths, drawn toward an abyss of the unknown. A shiver raced up her spine as desire coiled hot and gnawing in the pit of her stomach.

"Actually," Mace said, breaking the spell his eyes had cast over her, "in spite of the night's warmth, there was a severe chill in my room for a couple of hours last night."

Brianne glanced past him at Porthos.

The Musketeer smiled widely and raised his hands in a show of innocence. "We had a meeting."

She looked back at Mace.

"I suppose it was your ghosts, right?" he said, a derisive smile tugging at his lips.

"I did warn you the Tower Room was haunted," Brianne said. "But we'll understand if you'd like to cancel the rest of your stay, Mr. Calder. We can—"

"Call me Mace," he said, "and I have no intention of canceling the rest of my stay."

Lizbeth Raines smiled flirtatiously at him. "That's really an unusual name."

"It's Mason, but no one ever called me that but my mother." And his first fiancée, Mace thought, blocking out memories of Jaclyn Chellden.

"So, *chérie*," Christian said, taking one of the other empty chairs and looking at Brianne, "what is on the agenda for today? Are we to have a private tour?"

She placed her napkin on the table and pushed her chair back. "Perhaps tomorrow. Most of the homes in the area will be open for tours, however. Lafitte's Tavern in town serves a delicious festival lunch, and I'm sure you'll find most of the stores carry a wonderful selection of souvenirs. Then there's the pageant. Its first showing is tonight at nine."

"Oh, well, then can I take you to lunch?" Christian asked. "At the tavern?"

Brianne stood. "Thank you, but—"

"I've already invited Miss St. John to attend the festival with me," Mace said.

The cup of coffee Christian had been raising toward his lips stopped just short of its destination.

"I can join you for lunch, Christian," Lizbeth said, reaching across the table to pat his hand. "It should be fun."

Mace nearly choked trying not to laugh at the

wan smile that curved Christian's mouth at Lizbeth Raines's comment.

The fork on Lizbeth's plate suddenly flipped into the air, sending a large piece of eggs Benedict plopping down onto her lap.

She shrieked and jumped up. "Oh, look what I've done," she wailed, staring at the yellow sauce dripping down the front of her pale pink linen skirt. "How clumsy of me."

Brianne stared into the nothingness behind Lizbeth. The woman could have knocked that fork with her arm. A perfectly innocent accident. Then again . . .

Lizbeth sat back down. "Well, now I'll have to change before we go, but that will only take a minute."

The Winstons and Carfoiles excused themselves from the table and bid everyone a good day. They were going into town together.

Brianne followed them to the dining-room door and waved farewell. Mace stood and started to approach her as she looked back. "Have a good day in town," she said, glancing from him to Christian and Lizbeth, "and please let Mrs. Peel know if you won't be here for dinner this evening." With that, she turned and walked into the foyer.

Mace stepped out after her, only to see her disappear into another room. He stared at the tall door she'd closed behind her. Had he just been pointedly snubbed . . . or had she forgotten his invitation to attend the festival?

Never Alone

Brianne stepped into the study and leaned her back against the closed door behind her. She fought to get her temper under control, then looked around the room. It was decorated in soft ivory and varying shades of blue, ranging from the deepest to the lightest, but its drapes were still drawn, its windows closed. Normally the room had a soothing effect on her. But not now.

Her gaze scoured the room. She couldn't see *them*, but she could feel their presence. "Did you do that?" she snapped.

There was no response.

"I know you can hear me."

Something stirred on the floor beside the fireplace. She saw the corner of a silver-edged cloak peeking out from behind one of the tall wing chairs that faced the fireplace. She marched toward it. "Did you do that?"

Athos, sprawled on the floor, rolled onto his back and looked up at her, his bloodshot eyes still full of sleep. He pressed his knuckles into his temples and rubbed. "Would you mind speaking a little softer, *mon ange*?" he mumbled, his voice as heavy-sounding as his eyelids looked.

She turned to the French doors and drew back the drapes. "At the moment I am not in the mood to be an angel, Athos. Quite the contrary."

"*Bon Dieu*," he cursed, snapping his eyes shut and cringing away from the light. "What did I do to deserve this torture?"

Brianne threw open the doors to let some fresh

air into the room, then turned back to Athos. She knew that nothing she could do or say would make him feel better, so she didn't even try. There were three days every year that sent the tall, blond Musketeer spiraling into a wine bottle: the anniversary of his marriage to Lady de Winter, the date of the day he'd first rejected her, and the date of her death.

They had one more to go before the year was up.

"Are you okay?" she asked.

"As okay as a dead man can be," he grumbled, "with the sun burning his poor eyes and you screeching about like a put-upon charwoman."

"Thank you, I'll take that as a compliment, since you, at least, didn't say I looked like one, which I seem to remember you've had no problem doing in the past. Now"—she looked around the room as sunlight flowed through the open windows—"where are your friends?"

Athos stood and shrugged. "At the moment I truly don't know, but when I see them I'll warn them that you're looking for them."

Before she could say another word, he was gone.

Brianne settled into the chair behind her desk and reached for the phone. Hopefully the business at St. John Shipping was running a little more smoothly than the business at LeiMonte Castle.

"Ms. St. John's office."

"Trudy, it's me," Brianne said to the secretary

she'd inherited from Felix. "Has the fax from Broadelay come in yet?"

"No, but they called. Their attorney is changing something on the proposal, so it won't be here until this afternoon."

"Terrific. How am I supposed to approve the acquisition if they can't even get their demands together? Anything else I should know about?"

"No. Mr. Cummings said to tell you not to worry, everything's fine here."

"And don't hurry back," Brianne added.

Trudy laughed. "That's him."

After hanging up, Brianne rose, walked to the French doors, and looked out at the gardens. She raised a hand to her lips and touched them with her fingertips. The fire of Mace Calder's kiss was still there, burning into her every time she let herself remember it.

Brianne closed her eyes and leaned against the doorjamb. She had enough work to do to keep her busy most of the day, so why was she actually contemplating going into town with a man who stirred feelings inside her she had no time or desire for, and made her uncomfortable in more ways than one?

Mace decided to give up on the likelihood of Brianne's leaving the study for a while. He had a few calls to make and E-mails to answer anyway. Maybe when he was done, he'd try again to get her to give him a tour of the place or go into town with him. He turned toward the grand staircase and out of the corner of his eye caught a flash of something outside the study.

He paused to look more carefully, expecting to see Christian Deuvelle hugging the door and trying to think of some excuse to disturb Brianne, but no one was there. Mace frowned. He knew darned well he had seen something, and he didn't believe in ghosts.

Just then Serendipity dashed across the foyer toward the front door, pausing in front of it.

The cat. Of course.

Mace walked to the door and opened it.

Serendipity ran out without a backward glance.

"Well, don't say thank you," Mace said. He stepped out onto the porch.

Two peacocks sat at the edge of a sprawling carpet of lawn, just within the shadows of a giant live oak. Every branch on the massive tree was draped with Spanish moss, hanging like the tattered and rotting curtains that adorned some of the crumbling mansions he'd passed on his drive from New Orleans to Bayou de Joie. Other giant live oaks dotted the landscape, interspersed with magnolia, dogwood, myrtle, and chestnut.

The scene was very different from the one he was used to. His high-rise condo in San Francisco was all silver glass and concrete, the view of city buildings, the Golden Gate Bridge, and the bay.

He couldn't even remember if there were any trees in the vicinity. He hadn't paid any attention.

The roar of a bull gator broke the morning's silence, and Mace turned his attention toward the swamp beyond the manicured gardens.

That was one place he did not intend to go.

"Well, we're off," Lizbeth said, moving around Mace. She had a hand firmly clasped on Christian's arm. "Sure you don't want to join us?"

The usually smiling Christian looked sullen.

"No, thanks, you go ahead," Mace said. "Have fun."

They climbed into Lizbeth's small sports car and, moments later, drove down LeiMonte's long driveway and out of sight.

Mace went back into the house. The study door was open. Well, maybe he wouldn't have to kill time waiting for her after all. He approached the door, paused at the threshold, and looked inside. The room was empty.

Great. Now, where had she gone?

"Can I help you?" Brianne said, coming up behind him and holding a cup of coffee.

Mace smiled. "I was hoping we could go to the festival together."

His eyes caught hers, and Brianne felt suddenly flustered. She turned and walked into the room, feeling a need to put some space between them. "Well, I . . . um . . ."

Mace followed her.

"Tell him no," D'Artagnan said.

"*Oui*, he's not for you." Porthos preened in front of a mirror, seeing in its reflection what no one else could see but Brianne and Felix—his "physical" body. "Let him go alone if he wants to see the festival."

"I really do have work to—"

Mace took her hand and pulled her out onto the veranda. "You work too hard," he said softly, his deep, rich voice wrapping around her. "Take half a day. No, take the whole day and show me around Bayou de Joie and Barataria Bay. Then"—he looked deep into her eyes—"I'll take you to dinner or bring you back to your work, whichever you want."

"Tell him no, *mon coeur*, tell him no," D'Artagnan said.

"*Oui*, the last kind of man you need to be going out with is one who calls himself after a weapon," Porthos snapped. "Mace . . . hah! Why not Ax? Or Lance? Or even Cannon?"

Brianne turned a shocked gaze on the tall but still boyish-looking Musketeer, ready to tell him he was the last person who should be accusing someone else of being egotistical, when she remembered she wasn't alone. She turned to Mace.

"Don't you dare go," D'Artagnan commanded.

Brianne glanced at him.

Aramis suddenly appeared at D'Artagnan's side. "I agree with whatever it is D'Artagnan is telling you not to do."

Brianne glared at them. If it was up to them,

Never Alone

she'd never go out with anyone. She turned to Mace and smiled. "I'd love to go to the festival . . . and dinner."

"Wonderful."

"*Bon Dieu!*" D'Artagnan wailed, and threw up his hands.

"But I really do have some phone calls to make first."

"Fine, make them. I'll find something to occupy myself with until you're ready."

"We'll help him," Porthos said.

"No." The word was out of Brianne's mouth before she could stop it.

Mace, halfway out of the room, turned back. "No?"

She forced a smile to her lips. "I mean, I'll get my things and make the calls later. Just let me turn on my answering machine."

"He's wrong for you," D'Artagnan said.

"Definitely," Porthos agreed. "Look at those eyes."

Unable to help herself, Brianne glanced up from the machine and looked at Mace's eyes.

"Shifty, that's what they are," Porthos proclaimed. "Richelieu had eyes like that. Sneaky."

"A traitor's eyes," Aramis offered. "That's what they are."

"Yes, Richelieu eyes," D'Artagnan said, spitting the words out as if they were poison on his tongue.

"Will you stop!" Brianne snapped without thinking.

Mace, leaning against the door and waiting for her, instantly straightened. "Stop what?"

Brianne flushed. "Huh, nothing, I was . . . just trying to code my machine and it—"

"Cut off his head," Porthos cried. He drew his sword and jumped in front of Mace, slashing it back and forth wildly.

Brianne gasped.

Mace felt a rush of cool air sweep past his face.

EIGHT

Mace looked at the harlequin dancing down the street, followed closely by a polar bear wearing a purple top hat, and a huge red bean with white legs and gloved arms.

A group of men, faces painted and costumes straight out of a jungle, danced past, one banging on a huge drum.

Right behind them was a bevy of Las Vegas showgirls . . . except they weren't girls.

A pirate, a cowgirl, and a huge bumblebee walked behind the "showgirls," followed by several Confederate soldiers on horseback and a woman whose hoop skirt was so wide, it nearly took up the entire width of the street.

Music of a kind he'd never heard before blared from a nearby store, a mime gyrated atop a wooden box, and an old woman stood on one corner yelling "pra-leenes" while holding out something toward passersby that looked like a nut-topped pancake.

"They're candies," Brianne said, noticing Mace's frown of puzzlement. She bought two and handed him one. "Try it."

He bit into it. "Tastes like pure brown sugar," he said.

She smiled. "Almost."

He slipped the rest of the praline back into its little paper envelope and into the pocket of his shirt. "Does everyone always get this crazy during your festival?"

A miniature Chinese pagoda swayed past them, tripped on a curb, and fell to the ground with a resounding crash. Its occupant's legs flailed wildly as he yelled for help and tried to get up.

Brianne laughed. "Yes," she said, and hurried to help the pagoda to his feet. "It's kind of like our version of Mardi Gras. Smaller but just as colorful."

"A flower for your lady?"

Mace turned to look at the woman who'd tugged on the rolled-up sleeve of his white shirt.

She was the ugliest old crone he'd ever seen; stooped, with a large hump on her back, gray scraggly hair peeking out from beneath a ragged bandanna, and a wrinkled rubber face with a huge nose topped by a big, black wart.

She pulled a red rose from the basket of flowers dangling from one arm and offered it to Mace. "A flower for your lady?" she squeaked in a raspy, weak voice.

He took the flower.

"Five bucks," the woman said, her tone much stronger, her hand out.

"Five bucks?" he repeated. "For one flower?"

"Five bucks," she said again, and thrust her outstretched hand nearly into his chest. "Unless your lady ain't worth it, sonny."

Mace looked at Brianne, who was trying not to grin, and dug into his pocket. After the woman shuffled off, he handed the rose to Brianne.

"You didn't have to buy it," she said, and chuckled. "But I'm glad you did. That was Mrs. Devereaux, Bayou de Joie's librarian. The flowers are from her own garden."

"So what's she doing," Mace said with a sneer, "raising money for her tour of Europe?"

"Last year she made enough money from selling her flowers at the festival to buy two computers for the children's section of the library. I think this year she's going after a color printer."

"Oh." He felt like a heel. "Well, would you like to flog me now for my stupid comment, or should we have dinner first?"

Brianne sniffed the rose. "You bought the flower even though you had no way of knowing it was for a good cause. I don't really think a flogging is in order."

Mace smiled. "Good, I'm not big on pain. Now, where can we have dinner?"

She glanced at her watch. "Oh, it's getting late. Maybe I should get back. I mean, I didn't tell Mrs. Peel I wouldn't be home for dinner, and I do have—"

Mace held up his hands, as if in surrender. "I know, work to do."

Brianne laughed, then looked at him for a long moment. She couldn't deny that she'd had a wonderful time with him that afternoon. In fact, she couldn't remember when she'd enjoyed the festival more. But she also couldn't deny that several times when she'd looked at Mace, she had felt a flash of déjà vu, yet he had told her he'd never been to Louisiana before, and she'd never been to California. He was allegedly a stranger, but something told her that he wasn't. As quickly as the feeling assailed her, however, it disappeared.

"I'm not dangerous," Mace said, breaking into her thoughts, though the moment he said it, he knew it was an outright lie. He had meant the comment as an innocent jest, but as he'd heard his own words he'd realized just how deceptive they were. He was probably the most dangerous foe she'd ever face . . . she just didn't know it.

Mischief danced in Brianne's eyes. "And just how many women have you used that line on?"

"None."

She stared up at him, suddenly sober. "I'm not sure that's a compliment."

His hand wrapped gently around her upper arm, and he leaned toward her. "It is."

The breath caught in her throat as she realized he was going to kiss her, right there on the crowded street.

His lips brushed over hers, a featherlight touch that sent flames of heat swirling through her body and robbed her of breath. She swayed into him.

At that moment something bumped into her from the rear. She shrieked and fell hard into Mace.

"Oh, sorry," someone mumbled.

Mace and Brianne turned to look at what had to be the sorriest-looking horse in the world standing a few feet away. It took off its head and a young man smiled. "Hope I didn't hurt you. Hard to see where I'm going in this thing."

"You?" his rear end squawked. "What about me?"

The horse's belly suddenly split in two and a young woman appeared, straightening and shaking out her long hair. "All I can see from inside this thing is your tush." She suddenly saw Brianne and Mace staring at her and blushed. "Oh, geez, sorry." She punched her partner. "Why didn't you tell me there was someone here?"

He cringed playfully. "Well, I didn't think—"

"Oh, come on, we're going to be late for the contest."

The man apologized again, put his horse's head back on, and the woman reattached herself to his rear.

"Hey," he said, and jumped slightly as they walked away, "no pinching."

Brianne laughed and impulsively decided she didn't want the day to end just yet. She turned and looked down the street. "How about Jimbolee's?" She pointed to what looked like a private home, and one that had to be among the oldest in the city. "It has terrific food and a veranda out back that overlooks the bayou. I'll call Mrs. Peel."

"Sounds perfect." Mace tucked her arm through his and they walked toward the small restaurant. He rejected the first table they were shown to and pointed to another. "There," he said, "the one beneath the tree."

The table was set a little apart from the others. The gnarled and twisted boughs of a giant live oak created a canopy overhead, and the still waters of the bayou that edged Barataria Bay were barely a yard from the table.

After they ordered, Mace rose. "I'll be right back." He disappeared into the house, and Brianne turned to look out at the bayou. The heady fragrance of its flowers seemed to blend with the tantalizing odors wafting out from the kitchen to create a thoroughly soul-taunting scent.

The waning sun threw steep shadows over the landscape, and the bayou's night creatures began to stir, their sounds like a primeval symphony against the night.

She saw a nutria run across the fallen stump of a

tree and slip into the dark waters, barely disturbing the lilies that floated atop the surface.

Mace returned carrying a small candelabra. "I saw this in the reception room when we came in and decided to borrow it." He put the candelabra down on the table and lit its three white candles.

Brianne looked across the table at him as he retook his seat. Candlelight danced upon the dark strands of his hair like blue-black waves, but it was the look in his eyes that held her mesmerized. Shadows hovered within those blue depths, swirling slowly, beckoning to her, while at the same time warning her away. Devilry lived there, that had been more than evident to her all day, but now, as she looked deeper, she thought she sensed something else a hint of pain, a shade of loneliness.

She suddenly remembered the Musketeers warning her against Mace and wondered if they knew something she didn't.

"You're a million miles away," Mace said, interrupting her thoughts.

They had proceeded halfway through their dinner without speaking.

She looked up. "Sorry."

"Where were you?"

She shrugged, not wanting to tell him the truth. "Mars, Venus, who knows?" she said flippantly, and smiled. "Tell me something about yourself.

Does your family all live in the San Francisco area?"

"No. I was actually raised in a little town a few miles above Fort Worth called Dry Gulch."

"Dry Gulch?" Brianne laughed. "I don't believe you. That sounds like something straight out of the movies."

"My parents own a ranch there, run a few hundred head of cattle, but mostly they breed and raise quarter horses."

"Really? You're a cowboy." Brianne was amazed. "I never would have believed it."

"No. I'm an investment counselor who just happens to have been raised on a ranch."

"Do you go back much?"

"I go home for about a month every year to help my dad during foaling season, replenish my body with my mother's home cooking, and make sure my grandmother is behaving herself."

"Your grandmother?"

"Yeah. She's part Comanche, part Scottish, part French, and a little . . . different. Thinks she can tell the future," he added, seeing her curiosity. Even so, his explanation was putting it mildly. Selene Moran claimed to be clairvoyant, but most people, including half her family, thought she was just crazy. She was opinionated, outspoken, nosy, and totally disapproved of what Mace, her only grandchild, did for a living, as well as where he lived, and whom he associated with. Especially Jaclyn and Stephanie. So when she'd called him unexpectedly the day before his departure for New Orleans, he'd been surprised. She had never done that before. She'd said he should be extra careful this trip and should pay attention to his feelings, and he figured she had just been off playing with her daydreams again, so he humored her by saying he'd be careful, and promised to visit soon.

The waitress appeared and took their dishes. Mace picked up his wineglass with one hand and reached across the table with the other, placing it on top of Brianne's.

"Your grandmother sounds intriguing. How old is she?"

"Seventy-three going on five hundred and ten," he replied. His thumb moved slowly over her knuckles, a sensuous caress that sent shivers dancing up her arm.

"Where . . . where do you live?" Brianne said, wanting to pull her hand out of his, and wanting to leave it there forever.

"I have a condo in San Francisco and an office a few blocks away."

He spoke low, his deep voice playing over her nerve endings. Another wave of shivers raced over her skin while rivers of heat swept through her blood.

Brianne glanced down at her hand cradled in his. "Are you happy?" She looked up, shocked that she'd had the audacity to ask such a question.

Mace's dark eyes bored into hers. "Are *you* happy?"

She forced her gaze toward the bayou and tried to ignore both the feel of his caressing thumb and the rapid pounding of her heart. "Well, I don't like having to spend the week in New Orleans and only come home to LeiMonte on weekends, but it can't be helped. Felix is too old to keep up the pace of full-time work."

The sound of her uncle's name slashed through Mace's mind like a bolt of lightning, reminding him of why he was really at LeiMonte, his real purpose for getting close to Brianne St. John.

"Well, look who's here!"

Brianne and Mace both turned at the unmistakable voice of Christian Deuvelle.

"Isn't this something? We were dining inside and just noticed you two out here."

Brianne smiled at Christian and Lizbeth.

Mace glared.

"I asked the waitress if you two had ordered dessert yet, and when she said no, well, Lizbeth and I decided to order some for all of us."

Christian no sooner finished his announcement than the waitress appeared, pushing a brass serving cart, four bowls of vanilla ice cream set to one side of its top. Flipping this open, she struck a match and the cart's contents immediately turned to flame.

"Cherries jubilee," Christian exclaimed gaily, throwing an arm out toward the cart as if announcing that Elvis had just made an appearance. Dragging two chairs to their table, he and Lizbeth sat down. Christian moved his chair nearer to Brianne's. "Isn't this grand?"

"Just peachy," Mace said with a snarl, wondering if he were going to be able to get through the rest of his time at LeiMonte and accomplish what he needed to without murdering Christian Deuvelle.

NINE

A rush of cold air slapped Mace's cheek and he paused on LeiMonte's entry porch, startled. He rubbed the stinging flesh. If he didn't know better, he would have sworn Brianne had just slapped him.

She opened the front door and stepped over the threshold. "That really was a nice day. I don't remember when I've enjoyed the—"

The door immediately slammed behind her.

Brianne jumped and spun around, annoyed that he'd slammed the door, then surprised to see that she was standing in the foyer alone.

Serendipity trotted out from the parlor and curled her warm, silky body around one of Brianne's ankles.

Outside, Mace grabbed the doorknob, but it refused to turn.

"All right, which one of you locked him out?" Brianne snapped, looking around the room.

Never Alone

A whisper of a chuckle echoed softly.

She grabbed the doorknob, then shrieked and jerked her fingers away from the icy silver globe. It was so cold, it had nearly burned her flesh.

The knob rattled from the outside. "Brianne?" Mace banged a fist against the door. "Brianne?" He stopped and a deep frown dug into his brow. What the hell had he done to get the door slammed in his face?

Nothing, he decided. Maybe it had been a freak gust of wind. He stared at the door. So why wouldn't it open?

"Let him in," Brianne ordered, her voice barely above a whisper but harsh with anger.

"Whatever is the problem down there?" Christian called. "Is something wrong?"

Brianne turned to see the Frenchman standing on the staircase and staring down at her. Just what she didn't need.

He started down.

At the same moment Serendipity started up.

Mace banged on the door and called her again.

Christian saw the cat and dodged left.

"Dippy, no," D'Artagnan called out, realizing what was about to happen.

Too late.

The cat dodged right.

Christian's foot came down on her tail and Serendipity's screech filled the foyer.

Startled, Brianne nearly went through the ceiling.

The cat sped back down the stairs and huddled behind Brianne's legs, glaring out at Christian.

"Do things like that to the Englishman," D'Artagnan said, bending down eye to eye with Serendipity, "not to Deuvelle."

The cat hissed.

Christian glanced at Serendipity. "Sssss, to you too," he said, his face squirreled into a scowl of displeasure. He looked back up at Brianne. "Is there some reason you're not letting Calder in?"

Brianne bristled. He almost seemed happy about what was happening. And he obviously wasn't an animal lover. "No," she said. "The door accidentally slammed shut after I came in, and now it seems to be stuck." With a little help from some troublesome Musketeers, she added silently, turning to glare about the foyer again.

"Well, here, let me try," Christian said, trying to keep the irritation he felt from his voice. He'd been in the process of searching one of the upstairs sitting rooms and had hoped to finish before she came back. Now that was out of the question.

Brianne thought she could actually see Christian puff up with a sense of importance as he hurried past her and reached for the doorknob. She admonished herself for being snide. Just because he kept making passes at her and didn't take the hint that she wasn't interested was no reason for her to be derisive. "Be careful," she said hurriedly, suddenly apprehensive for him. "It may be—"

He grabbed the door handle, turned the knob, and jerked the door open.

Mace, who at the same time had braced himself against the door, turned the knob, and pushed with his shoulder, practically fell into the room. He stumbled across the foyer and tripped over Serendipity.

The cat screeched loudly and ran to hide behind Brianne's legs again.

Mace grabbed the staircase newel post and barely managed to keep himself from falling flat on his face.

Straightening, he spun around to face Brianne. "What the . . ." He'd been about to demand an explanation as to why she'd slammed the door in his face then locked it, but the words stuck in his throat when he caught sight of Christian. He had one hand on the doorknob and a smile on his face that was so smug, it set Mace back a moment. If Brianne was going to do a sudden about-face on him and say she'd had a horrible day in his company and thought he was a jerk, he didn't want to hear it in front of the flying Frenchman.

"Sorry," Brianne said, "I guess a draft must have slammed it shut behind me."

A draft named Christian Deuvelle? Mace wondered, but kept the suspicion to himself. He nodded. "Yeah, old houses are pretty drafty." He looked down at Serendipity. "Is she okay?"

Brianne nodded. "She would be better if she

learned to stop being in everyone's way, wouldn't you, Dippy?"

The cat threw her a haughty glance, flicked her tail, and pranced toward the stairs.

Brianne chuckled and looked back at Mace. She suddenly didn't want what had been an enjoyable day to end on such an uncomfortable note. "I . . . ah . . . would you like some coffee?"

Mace smiled. "That would be nice." He turned to the other man. "Well, thanks and good night, Christian," he said pointedly.

Christian's eyes narrowed and his lips twisted into a sneer of unhappiness, but the look cleared and was replaced with a smile the moment Brianne glanced his way.

"Yes, thank you, Mr. Deuvelle," she said.

Christian walked stiffly across the foyer and hurriedly climbed the stairs. "Thanks," he mumbled mockingly under his breath. If he'd had half a brain, he would have left Mace Calder standing outside until hell froze over.

"We should have asked him to join us," Brianne said, feeling guilty at having slighted one of LeiMonte's guests.

"No, we shouldn't have." Mace grinned.

The devilish gleam that sparkled from his dark eyes captivated her.

"Careful," D'Artagnan whispered, his warm breath flowing through the long strands of hair that cascaded over Brianne's ear. "He's dangerous."

"A rogue," Porthos added.

She ignored them and forced a smile to her lips. "Why don't you go on into the parlor, Mace, and I'll see if Mrs. Peel is still up and will fix us some coffee. Otherwise I'll do it and be back in a few minutes." She turned and walked hastily into the kitchen. It was empty, Mrs. Peel having evidently retired for the night, but there was a full pot of coffee sitting on the stove as well as a plate of cookies nearby. Brianne stopped in the center of the room. "Okay, where are you?" she snapped, her temper flaring. "Come on. I want to see you. All four of you. Right now!"

No one appeared.

"Now!" Brianne snapped again.

"Not while you're in this mood," D'Artagnan said.

She whirled, looking for him, but he was nowhere in sight. "Coward."

He chuckled. "My sainted mother always warned me that the most formidable foe I could ever meet was not a soldier on the field of battle, but an angry woman."

"Did she also teach you to be absolutely incorrigible? And to mind other people's business?"

He laughed again. "No. I got the first from my father, the second from my older sisters."

"Terrific family," Brianne grumbled.

"Yes, they were." He sighed wistfully.

A flash of guilt assailed Brianne at the hint of melancholy in his tone. She straightened her shoulders and walked to the counter, pouring two cups of coffee. "You can't do things like that to him," she said, calmer now. She picked up the tray with the coffee and cookies and turned toward the door. "Please. He's a guest."

"He's trying to be more," Aramis observed.

She stopped and looked to her left, in the direction from which his voice had come, but the only things she saw were the refrigerator and the door to the pantry.

"So you intend to keep this up?" she prodded.

No one answered.

She knew suddenly that they were gone. A sense of uneasiness seized her. Mace. She pushed open the kitchen's swinging door and hurried across the foyer toward the parlor. There were no screams or sounds of panic, but that didn't mean anything; they could have gagged him. She practically ran into the room, fully expecting to see Mace Calder hanging from the chandelier, or wrapped up tight in the drapes. Instead he was sitting quietly in one of the wing chairs that faced the fireplace and flipping idly through the pages of a magazine.

Soft strains of music flowed from a tall, mirror-fronted armoire that housed Felix's state-of-the-art stereo system. Obviously Mace had turned it on. Brianne released a sigh of relief.

Noticing her in the doorway, he rose. "Here, let me take that."

"No, really, it's all—"

Mace took the tray.

She waited, holding her breath and expecting the tray to fly out of his arms and into his face. Don't, she prayed. Please, don't.

Mace set the tray on the small, marble-topped table situated before a Louis XIV settee.

Again Brianne breathed a sigh of relief. "Thank you," she whispered.

Mace heard. Straightening, he smiled. "You're welcome."

She hadn't been talking to him, but she wasn't going to tell him that. Brianne took a seat on the settee and picked up her coffee cup. "It really was a nice day. . . ."

Serendipty jumped onto the settee and sat down between them.

Mace laughed. "I don't think she wants us to get too close."

Serendipity suddenly crouched toward Brianne and seemed to glare at Mace.

"She's pretty skittish around strangers, and now that she's about to become a new mama, she's worse."

Mace shrugged. "My mother had a cat when I was a kid. Pure black and scared of her own shadow. Even after ten years of living with us, we'd have to get down on our knees and coax her for a good five minutes before she'd come near." He stretched a hand out slowly toward Serendipity. "Come on, girl," he said softly. "No one's going to hurt you."

The cat's tail flicked rhythmically as she

watched Mace, but she made no effort to sniff his outstretched fingers.

"Good girl," D'Artagnan whispered softly into the cat's ear.

Mace gave up and relaxed against the back of the ornately designed settee and, sipping on his coffee, turned his attention back to Brianne.

"You're staring," Brianne said a minute later. Goose bumps danced across her flesh beneath the seductive heat she recognized in his gaze.

"Sorry," Mace mumbled, but he didn't stop. It had just occurred to him that it had been hours since he'd thought about business, and his real reason for being at LeiMonte. It should bother him, but somehow it didn't. He set the coffee cup down and reached for Brianne's hand.

Suddenly Serendipity jumped up and lashed out with extended claws, hissing wildly.

Mace snatched his hand back, but not quickly enough. A line of red appeared across his skin.

"Bravo, Dippy!" D'Artagnan and Porthos yelled, both suddenly materializing on the other side of the coffee table.

Brianne glared at them. "Go away."

"She's okay," Mace said. "It was my fault. I moved too quick and scared her."

Brianne looked back at him. "Oh, I didn't . . . I mean . . ." Her gaze dropped to his hand. "You're hurt."

He smiled. "I'll live."

"Unfortunately," Porthos said.

Brianne rose. "I'll get some antiseptic." She hurried toward the kitchen. One of the cabinets in the pantry was well stocked with medical supplies. "Can I have some privacy?" she snapped as she looked for the antiseptic. "Is that really too much to ask? For just a little privacy in my life?"

"He's dangerous," D'Artagnan again warned.

"He has shifty eyes," Porthos added.

Brianne whirled around. "You have shifty suspicions!" She turned back and grabbed the bottle of antiseptic, then stalked toward the door.

"We all agree," Porthos called after her. "He's wrong for you."

"Oh, go haunt something in the swamp for a while," she threw over her shoulder.

Brianne stopped in the doorway to the parlor and stared at Mace, who was standing before one of the French doors across the room. "How did you do that?"

He glanced up and smiled as he continued to stroke the back of the large white cat cradled in his arms. "Oh, we just had a little talk."

"A talk?" Brianne echoed, opening the bottle as she approached. Screwing up her face in mock disbelief, she stared at the cat. "Dippy, is that really you?"

The cat purred.

"Amazing." She marveled. "I've never seen her respond to anyone that way. It normally takes a person days just to get to the point where she doesn't hiss at them." She soaked a cotton swab with antiseptic and pressed it to the scratch on the back of Mace's hand.

Serendipity's head instantly went up as the acrid smell permeated the air. Her nose wiggled, her eyes narrowed, and with a growl of dissatisfaction deep in her throat, she pushed away from Mace and jumped to the floor. With tail twitching, she pranced from the room.

"I thought she'd never leave," Mace said, a teasing note in his deep, husky voice. Before Brianne had a clue to his intentions, he took the antiseptic bottle and cotton swab from her hand, set them on a nearby table, and swung her into his arms. Crushing her body to his, he began to dance her slowly around the room.

For a fleeting instant she thought of pulling away from him, but the urge was gone almost before she'd acknowledged it. She could feel his warm breath against her cheek, his strong hand pressed securely to the small of her back. As the moments passed, the music played, and the warmth of the night air drifted in through the open French doors, she became even more conscious of him; of the faint scent of his cologne, the sleek muscles hidden beneath the well-tailored clothes, the slight raggedness of his breath and beat of his heart.

Her body suddenly felt as if a thousand flames had just been ignited in her bloodstream. She looked up at him, afraid of the feelings coursing through her. She was adept at her work, confident in the world of business, but the feelings that overwhelmed her as he held her in his arms were too overpowering, too frightening.

They caused her to lose control, and she couldn't allow herself that. She had too many responsibilities. Yet she had no will to stop what was happening.

Mace paused, his eyes meeting hers. Reality narrowed to the scope of their gazes. Everything around them disappeared.

The game was fire. Hot, dangerous, even lethal.

Mace knew that he should let her go, turn and run, put as much distance between himself and Brianne St. John as he could, but he also knew it was too late. The attraction between them was more than just sexual. He hadn't wanted to admit that, but there was no way left him to deny it. The desire that had ignited within him the moment they had met, the raw need that had been gnawing at him from the moment he'd walked through the doors of LeiMonte and seen her, were not welcome, yet somehow seemed inevitable.

He'd never felt so much, so deeply, for a woman so quickly, and it scared him.

Once before he'd let his heart rule his actions, and he'd been plunged headfirst into disaster.

Mace lowered his head and brushed his lips across hers, surrendering—inviting—the inevitable.

TEN

His lips caressed hers in a whisper of a touch, teasing and elusive, leaving delicious sensations behind on her skin wherever they roamed.

Waves of shock swept through Brianne's body, rippling endlessly and filling her with reckless abandon. Her hands slipped up over the broad expanse of his chest and moved behind his neck.

His arms tightened about her as his lips painted hers with fire and his tongue explored the recesses of her mouth.

The hunger of his kiss shattered any calm or resistance still left within her. Slow and thoughtful, then swift and urgent, it was everything she'd ever dreamed a kiss could be. She drank in its sweetness, wanting it never to stop, reveling in this man's savage demand, cherishing his tender caress. What little sanity still huddled within her mind instantly vanished as his lips deserted hers and seared a burning path down her neck.

She felt her knees weaken, her nipples harden, and the gnawing ache in her loins threaten to explode. Sensations she'd never been aware she could experience, feelings she had never been aware even existed, assailed her, one after another. But most urgent of all was the need for him not to stop.

His lips sketched a series of slow, shivery kisses along the curve of her shoulder, then swiftly returned to claim her mouth in a smoldering kiss that stirred her to the very reaches of her soul.

This was what she had always wanted, this was what she had unknowingly been waiting for all of her life. Nothing else existed, nothing mattered but this tall, dark man who was holding her in his arms, whose mouth was wreaking havoc with her senses and inciting a passion that threatened to overwhelm her. And she welcomed it.

Suddenly the CD player made a horrendous screeching sound and ground to a halt.

At the same time the French doors slammed shut and a small Boston fern sitting in an eighteenth-century vase on the fireplace mantel crashed to the floor.

Brianne jerked out of Mace's arms.

Mace looked around, startled by the interruption. "What the hell was that?"

As if in answer, and for good measure, the door to the foyer slammed open, several framed pictures sitting on an end table slapped facedown, and the fireplace utensils crashed onto the marble hearth.

"Stop it!" Brianne said loudly.

One of the chairs bounced off the floor.

A table rocked, nearly hurling the crystal lamp sitting on it to the floor.

One of the French doors flew open again.

"Not till you do," a chorus of voices rang out softly.

Brianne clenched her fists, not about to let *them* win. If they did, she knew she would forever be at their mercy. "Stop it! Stop it right now, or I swear I'll run off and marry him!"

The room suddenly became deathly still.

"Thank you."

She turned back to Mace and found him staring at her, a deep frown digging into his brow.

"I told you LeiMonte was haunted."

"And you were what, threatening to run away with me and then thanking your ghosts for stopping their tirade when they didn't like that idea?"

"Something like that."

Mace chuckled. "Well, I guess it's not very complimentary toward me, but it's great stuff for your publicity brochures. Inventive, too, turning a minor earthquake into a haunting incident, though you don't have to try to sell me on the idea. I don't believe in that stuff, remember?"

He looked around the room. "But, compared with a couple of quakes I've experienced in San Francisco, this one was pretty mild."

She didn't feel like arguing. "Think what you like."

He reached out for her.

Brianne jerked away. "No."

Mace frowned.

"I'm sorry," she said. So many emotions were warring within her—anger, desire, frustration, joy, fear—she knew it was too dangerous to remain with him any longer. "Let's just say good night." She walked to the door, then paused and looked back. "Thank you for a lovely day, Mace. I really did enjoy myself."

The problem was, Mace thought, so had he.

For the entire next day Brianne kept herself sequestered in LeiMonte's large study, doing a balancing act between the phones, her calculator, a laptop computer, and the fax machine. The proposal from Broadelay still hadn't shown up at the office, which meant the acquisition of that company was a lot further down the road than she'd anticipated. A minor problem, but luckily, with a few scheduling changes, a solvable one. Though time was running out.

As the large grandfather clock in the foyer struck five, Brianne sat back in her chair and stretched. A half-dozen ledgers lay open on her desk, along with several piles of letters, balance sheets, and departmental budget proposals.

Not until that moment had she realized that the

fractious four hadn't made an appearance all day. Obviously they were satisfied that she was not going to cross them and fall into the arms of Mace Calder again.

Either that, or they were off planning a counterattack.

A knock on the door interrupted her thoughts. Mrs. Peel opened the door and stuck her head into the room. "About time you got ready for your party, don't you think?"

Brianne's mouth dropped open in shock. "Party? Is that tonight?"

The housekeeper nodded.

"Oh, cripes," Brianne swore, "I forgot. Where's Uncle Felix?"

"Putting on his tux." Mrs. Peel smiled. "I expect he'll be hollering any minute for me to come up and fix his tie and cummerbund."

Christian glanced over his shoulder toward the door of the old nursery. The room hadn't been mentioned in any of the documents he'd studied on LeiMonte, so he hadn't even known it existed until he'd accidentally found it only a few moments earlier. It would make a perfect hiding place, hidden away in the middle of the servants' quarters as it was, but so far he'd found nothing.

Hearing nothing more in the hallway, he turned back to the bookshelf he'd been examining and brushed a finger against its back wall.

"*Nom d'une pipe*, what is he doing?" Porthos wondered aloud, leaning over Christian's shoulder to stare at the wall he was knocking his finger against.

Athos shrugged. "Looking for a hidden stairwell?"

D'Artagnan walked into the room and the two Musketeers turned toward him. "The parlor is wall-to-wall with people," he grumbled.

"This one is knocking against the wall," Porthos said.

"Maybe he thinks someone is in there," Athos offered.

D'Artagnan turned a piercing eye on Christian and moved to look at what he was doing. "For the moment Brianne is safe," he said. "But I suggest we find out what this one is up to."

"Where's Aramis?" Athos asked.

"Downstairs feasting his eyes on the women, where else?" D'Artagnan said, walking through the wall and into the hallway.

Mace stood near the French doors in the drawing room and stared out at the slowly sinking sun. He hadn't had a good day, and he was irritable. Once he'd realized Brianne was not going to be around for most of the day, he'd decided to do some work of his own, but for the most part concentration had eluded him. What galled him was the thought that she had probably done just fine not thinking about him most of the day, while thoughts of her had been torturing him constantly ever since she'd walked out of the room the night before. She'd left him nearly strangling in his own desire and more in need of a cold shower than he'd ever been in his entire life.

His daily call to Melanstrup that morning had nearly ended in disaster when the man said something and Mace had been too preoccupied with daydreams of Brianne to listen or answer. Melanstrup was not exactly known for his patience.

Mace glanced across the crowded room. Almost every notable person in Bayou de Joie had come to LeiMonte for its annual "festival dinner party." He would have preferred to be anywhere else, but at least he'd managed to get his libido under control and his thoughts well sectioned, situated, and sorted.

His trip to LeiMonte was for one purpose and one purpose only: to gather the information that would permit Melanstrup to carry out his plan. If he had to use Brianne St. John to accomplish that goal, then he would do so. But that's all there would be to it; a little pleasure to spice up business. He didn't want or need another woman in his life. His attraction to Brianne St. John was purely physical. Sex and lust, that was it. She wasn't even his type. She was alluring, attractive, intriguing: he couldn't deny that, but he didn't usually like business-minded women.

A movement by the door caught his eye and he

turned. Brianne stood in the doorway, her gaze settled upon him.

Mace felt a shock wave move through his body, immobilizing him—invigorating him. The soft light of the chandelier played upon her face, danced within the red-gold tangle of her hair, and sparkled off the sapphire sequins that covered her form-fitting, floor-length gown.

The full impact of her beauty and the depth of his desire for her hit him dead center. A torrent of need raced through his body with the force of a hurricane, threatening to turn calm emotional seas into tidal waves of hungry passion.

The game he was playing had suddenly turned threatening, but he had no choice but to keep on with it. He turned back to the bar to regain his composure and cool his ardor, and to pour her a glass of wine.

Brianne had purposely paused in the doorway, not for effect, but to give herself a moment to see who had already arrived for Felix's annual gathering. At least that's what she tried to tell herself. That her gaze immediately sought and found Mace Calder gave the lie to that theory, and realizing this unnerved her.

"Ah, Brianne." A short, portly man paused before her. "Everything is grand, as usual."

She smiled at the mayor of Bayou de Joie but her gaze never left Mace. The mayor finally drifted away to talk to someone else and Mace turned toward the bar.

Brianne took in the way the silken threads of his tuxedo defined the lean and well-honed lines of his body, while the white of his shirt accentuated the rich, bronzed sheen of his skin.

She wanted to run to him, but she didn't move.

There was something about Mace Calder that sent blasts of alarm echoing through her thoughts. At the same time there was an unexplainable yearning in her to be close to him, a need to touch him, be touched by him.

She took another step into the ballroom, and as if sensing her movement, Mace turned back toward her, their eyes meeting again. He crossed the room, moving easily and steadily through the cluster of people that separated them, and paused before her. She was too much of a vision to resist tonight, and in spite of the vow he'd made earlier—to keep his mind on business no matter what he was doing, even with her—business was the furthest thing from his thoughts. He offered her the glass of wine, then he raised his glass in toast.

"To?" Brianne asked softly, her gaze holding his.

"Us."

Aramis slapped his cloak over one shoulder and whirled around to face his cohorts. "D'Artagnan, we really need to get back downstairs. There's no telling what is happening down there that shouldn't be."

D'Artagnan glanced at his friend.

"You merely want to ogle the ladies some more," Porthos said, and laughed.

Aramis straightened, indignant. "I do not ogle," he snapped.

"What we need to do," D'Artagnan said calmly, "is find out what our friend Deuvelle is really up to." He turned away from Christian's suitcase and shoved a hand into his garment bag.

"Maybe he's just examining the place," Athos offered. "He is an art dealer, after all."

D'Artagnan shook his head. "He's knocking on walls, looking up fireplace flues, inspecting ceiling moldings and windowsills. None of that has anything at all to do with art."

"Damn, and I'd hoped he was the one for Brianne." Aramis grimaced.

"He'd at least have been better than that Englishman," D'Artagnan snapped.

"Richelieu eyes," Porthos spat.

"Bon Dieu," Athos said suddenly. He was staring at the name inscribed in a flourishing hand on the first page of the small journal he'd lifted out of Christian's briefcase—Comtesse de Winter.

ELEVEN

They were the last ones on the dance floor . . . the last ones left in the ballroom. As the small band Felix had hired played the night's final waltz, Mace whirled Brianne slowly, sensuously, across the gleaming hardwood floor, and finally out onto the terrace beyond the open French doors.

The night had been too perfect; she didn't want it to end, in spite of having spent nearly the entire time holding her breath and waiting for disaster to strike. But the Musketeers had never made an appearance, and there were no party crashers as there had been one year in the past, Christian Deuvelle had seemed content to spend most of the evening with Lizbeth Raines, and no one drank too much or made a scene.

The night's warm and humid air touched Brianne's bare shoulders, the heavy fragrance of the bayou invaded her breath, and the music ended, but Mace did not release her from the circle of his arms. A soft hum of voices and the clash of metal signaled that the band had begun to pack their instruments and was making ready to leave. He continued to hold her to him, gently cradled against his chest, a wall encased in white cotton, while one hand pressed into her back, warm and strong. Her body was all too aware of him, every fiber and muscle within her attuned to his every move. The distinct scent of him, a tantalizing mixture of man and cologne, had long ago invaded her senses, until now she knew that she would always associate that particular fragrance with Mace Calder.

She looked up at him and saw the same hunger that raged within her reflected in the dark pools of his blue eyes. The hard hammering of her heart and the ragged struggle of her lungs for breath intensified as his gaze slowly roamed her face.

From the moment he'd walked into LeiMonte and into her life, some deep instinct within her had been alerted to a danger she neither recognized nor understood. Now she didn't care. The barrage of emotions he aroused in her was too potent, too intense, for her to think of anything else . . . at least at the moment.

"What are you doing to me?" Mace whispered softly.

Feelings and sensations he neither welcomed nor had expected assailed him in ways he'd never experienced before. Nothing seemed to matter anymore but the woman he held in his arms, whose mere presence managed to erase every other care and thought from his head.

"Nothing different from what you're doing to me," Brianne said breathlessly, not even wondering where she'd gotten the courage to speak so boldly. With him it seemed natural. Right.

His embrace tightened around her, pinning her arms between them, her hands pressed flat to the silk lapels of his tuxedo. Brianne felt the touch of his lips as they brushed lightly over her own. Her arms moved to encircle his neck. His mouth captured hers in a tender caress that almost instantly turned to savage urgency.

As if in answer to the conquest of her lips, the blood within her veins turned to hot, spiraling waves of flame, melded with the maddeningly out-of-control beat of her heart, and flowed out again in fiery abandon. There was not even a thread of resistance left in Brianne, no hesitation or doubt. He had silently demanded her heart, and she had surrendered it willingly.

The world slipped away, quietly, thunderously, completely, disappearing into the darkness and light that whirled about her like a blinding tempest.

Whatever control Mace still maintained over his senses, whatever reins he still held over his emotions, it all vanished when her lips answered his kiss.

His tongue caressed and explored the deep

caverns of her mouth, and flicked against her tongue as it attempted to do the same. He seduced her senses.

She ravaged his.

Brianne leaned into him as he became all that existed for her, all that mattered in the sensual world into which his passion was pulling her.

"Brianne St. John," Porthos snapped. "*Bon Dieu*, I'm surprised at you."

She jerked away from Mace so fast, she nearly lost her balance.

Porthos stood, hands on hips, barely a hairbreadth away, and glared at her. "The minute we turn our backs, thinking you're safe in a house full of people, you go cavorting with this . . . this . . . Englishman!"

Brianne's temper flared as indignation swept over her.

"Yes, where is that uncle of yours?" Athos asked. "He should be watching over you, acting as chaperon."

Watch over her? She clenched her hands into fists. She'd tell them a thing or two about who should be watching whom!

"Not letting you get seduced by some shifty-eyed lothario," Aramis added, materializing on the musicians' dais.

That did it! The world's biggest lothario calling Mace Calder a lothario! She opened her mouth to give all three of them a piece of her mind when a short, ear-piercing screech echoed through the house.

"Oh, no!" Brianne spun around and ran into the foyer.

"What is it?" Mace asked.

She looked around frantically. "Dippy."

He frowned. "Dippy?"

"She did the same thing last year. She's looking for a place to have her kittens."

Another screech echoed down the grand staircase. Brianne grabbed the skirt of her gown and raced up the stairs with Mace at her heels.

The second-floor hallway was still and empty.

"Meowwwww!"

Brianne raced for the spiral stairs that led to the Tower Room. She stopped at the door.

Serendipity had dragged one of Mace's shirts into a corner and was kneading it into a nest.

"Oh, Dippy, not in here!" Brianne wailed. She ran to the cat and dropped to her knees, then glanced at Mace as he joined her on the floor.

Dippy had lain down and was growling softly.

"I hope that wasn't your best shirt."

Mace grinned. "I guess I've just made another donation to a good cause."

"Great, we'll make a brass plaque in your honor and remember you forever," D'Artagnan said, peering over Mace's shoulder. "Now you can go back to wherever you came from and leave us to our room."

Brianne threw D'Artagnan an annoyed glance.

An hour later six newborn kittens were squirming around on Mace's shirt while their mother busily cleaned them.

Brianne got back to her feet. "I'll go downstairs and find a basket or box or something to put them in, then take them to another room."

"Why?"

She turned, surprised, and stared at Mace. "Well, you don't want them in here."

"Why not?"

"Because it is not your room," D'Artagnan snapped.

"She picked this room for her nursery," Mace said, "so let her stay." He knelt down again and reached out to stroke Serendipity's head. "Anyway, I could use the company up here."

The cat began to purr and leaned her head into Mace's caressing finger.

Brianne smiled. He liked cats. And Dippy obviously liked him, unusual as that was. "Well, all right," she said, turning to leave the room, "if you're sure?"

He rose and smiled. "I'm sure."

She nodded. "Good night, then."

He joined her at the door, and before she could step out into the hallway, Mace dragged her back into his arms. His lips once again descended on hers.

A trembling weakness instantly spread through Brianne's veins.

Mace's lips left hers slowly. "Good night," he whispered. She opened her eyes and saw Athos and Aramis glaring at her from over Mace's left shoulder. D'Artagnan and Porthos glowered over his right.

Mace lay on the huge poster bed in his room and stared up at the ornate fabric of its canopy, not really seeing it. Instead, his attention was focused on the image of Brianne St. John that filled his memory as his mind replayed, over and over, the kiss they'd shared hours earlier.

What was there about her, he wondered, that got under his skin? Had him forgetting why he was there and thinking only of holding her in his arms, kissing her, making love to her?

Suddenly he felt as if he were being watched. The feeling crept over him slowly, like a wave moving over a sandy northern shore, cold, steady, and sure. Mace rose slightly away from the pillow and looked around the room, which was lit only by the glow from his open laptop's screen.

There was no one else in the room, which he'd already known. He glanced toward the windows. No one stared back at him from the other side of the glass—understandable since he was three stories off the ground with no balcony or stairs attached. Nevertheless he definitely felt as if he were being watched.

"So, what are we going to do?" Porthos asked, leaning against one of the ornately carved posts at the foot of Mace's bed. "Stand around here and watch her fall for *him*?" He pointed to Mace and spat out the last word as if it were the worst he'd ever said.

"Well, she certainly does seem to be doing that," Aramis said from beside him. "But, you know, even if he is a lothario, a lady's heart is fickle and—"

"You should know about fickle hearts," Porthos snapped, wheeling to face him. "And about being a lothario."

Aramis stiffened. "I beg your pardon."

"You can beg all you want, but it's still true that you were more renowned for your bedchamber skills than—"

Aramis whipped out his sword. "I never lost a duel."

"Oh?" Porthos spat. "And what about that time Richelieu's men had us surrounded at Marchant? If I hadn't been with you—"

"Arguing among ourselves isn't going to solve anything." D'Artagnan interrupted quietly from the opposite side of the bed.

"D'Artagnan's right," Athos said. He pushed away from the night table he'd been leaning a hip against and moved to stand beside the other Musketeer. "But the way I see it, there really isn't anything to solve. Brianne is falling for him and that's that."

Porthos puffed up like an angry rooster. "That's that? Well, maybe that's that for you," he said with a snarl, and thrust his sword across the bed as he pointed at Athos, "but there's still plenty I can do, and that does not include standing around morosely while she throws her life away on this shifty-eyed scoundrel!" He touched the tip of his sword to Mace's throat.

Mace felt something cold touch his Adam's apple. He coughed, then swallowed hard, but the sensation didn't go away. He pushed up from his pillow.

Porthos's sword slid right through his neck.

"Be careful!" D'Artagnan snapped.

Porthos grinned.

Mace cleared his throat again as the icy sensation intensified with his movement. He reached for the glass of water on the night table.

Porthos pulled the sword back and slid it into the scabbard hanging over his hip.

"If this had been one of your days," Athos snapped, "you'd have killed him."

"Damn." Porthos's face screwed up into a mask of disappointment, then his expression instantly changed to a grin. "Could I try again tomorrow?"

"Of course not," D'Artagnan said. He began to stroke his dark goatee as he fell into thought.

Never Alone

"Pity," Aramis murmured, shaking his head, "it would simplify matters."

"No, it wouldn't. She'd leave," Athos said. He looked around solemnly at the others. "Brianne would leave."

D'Artagnan nodded. "Yes, she would."

Porthos threw up his hands in exasperation. "Then what are we going to do?"

D'Artagnan turned to reread the message on the screen of Mace's computer.

```
Calder,
   Have discovered St. John
is in secret negotiations
with Broadelay. Imperative
you accomplish your task at
LeiMonte ASAP and return to
SF.
                            DM
```

"What we have always done," he finally said, quietly.

Porthos frowned. "What we have . . . ?"

D'Artagnan spun on his heel and disappeared through the wall.

The three remaining Musketeers stared at each other in confusion.

D'Artagnan's voice suddenly boomed through the room, summoning them. *"Venez."*

Mace settled back on the pillow, the icy sensation in his throat gone. But what the hell had it been? He looked around the room again, then chided himself. There were no such things as ghosts.

TWELVE

Along with the other guests, Brianne was already at the breakfast table when Mace walked into the dining room the next morning. He felt certain someone had sent a marching band parading through his head the previous night and the cymbal player seemed to have been left behind. He was still crashing his metal disks against Mace's temples.

He made straight for the coffeepot, squinting against the light flowing in through the room's windows. Two glasses of wine, that's all he'd had, but this hangover had to be the mother of all hangovers.

"Good morning, Mr. Calder," Brianne said.

Mace forced a smile. "Good morning." Though as far as he was concerned there was nothing good about it. His room had alternated between freezing cold and comfortable all night. Once he'd thought he heard voices and had been convinced Deuvelle had his radio on and turned up purposely so Mace wouldn't be able to sleep, and about three A.M. the cat had begun hissing and having a royal fit, batting her extended claws at the air and acting as if Satan himself were after her kittens.

He piled scrambled eggs, bacon, and toast on a plate and turned to the table.

Brianne rose the moment he sat down, her pulse racing erratically and her knees feeling a bit weak. "Please excuse me, everyone"—she smiled—"but I have a lot of work to do this morning."

"Oh, but I was hoping you'd lunch with me today," Christian said, rising hastily.

Brianne struggled to keep the disappointment from her face. She'd thought the man had given up. "I'm sorry, Mr. Deuvelle, but I really can't today." She looked at Lizbeth and let her brows rise in question. "But perhaps . . . ?"

"Yes," Lizbeth said quickly, "you and I can go, Christian. We'll lunch at that cute little restaurant we saw on Main Street and visit some of the shops we didn't get to yesterday."

Christian smiled wryly and sat down.

"Well, have fun," Brianne told them with as much sincerity as she could muster. She turned and walked toward the foyer, the memory of Mace's lips burning into hers taking up her thoughts and turning her blood to a volcanic flow that was leaving her feeling scorched and weak.

Mace watched her leave. After their kiss he'd

expected a little more than to be brushed off with the rest of the guests.

"Too bad, ol' boy," Porthos said, bending so that his mouth was only an inch from Mace's ear. He laughed gaily and slapped a hand on Mace's shoulder. "Too, too, too bad."

Mace flinched at the sudden sweep of cold air that settled upon his left shoulder and blew across his ear.

Brianne paused in the middle of the foyer and looked at the coffee cup she was holding. It was nearly empty. She looked back toward the dining room. She didn't want to go back in there, didn't want to look into his eyes again. But she did want another cup of coffee. She walked into the kitchen and saw that the pot on the burner was empty. Her shoulders stiffened as she spun around and marched toward the dining room. She was being silly. She was not going to let Mace Calder or anyone else keep her out of her own dining room. After all, this was her home.

As she crossed the hallway Serendipity jumped from the staircase and trotted into the dining room a few steps before her. The cat made a beeline to Mace, rubbing her body against his leg and purring loudly.

He bent and rubbed a knuckle over her head. "Hey, Dippy," he said, "taking a break from motherhood, huh?"

Serendipity twisted through his legs and rubbed against his ankles.

"Oh, Brianne, you've come back," Christian cooed. He rose from his place at the table and started toward her.

As he was speaking, Serendipity crossed his path on her way to Brianne, then stopped, turned, and glared at him, ears flat, back arched.

"Oh, no . . . shoo!" Christian waved his hands wildly at the cat. "Scat! Get away! *Fous le camp!* Shoo!"

Brianne paused and looked at Christian.

The cat took a step toward him.

"Go away," he ordered again, flinging his hands at her in a sweeping motion.

"Dippy," Brianne admonished.

The cat ignored her. Narrowing her eyes, she hunched her back and hissed at the Frenchman, swiping out with one paw.

Christian stepped back, eyes wide. "Oh! What was that for? Beastly animal."

"Dippy, go find your friends." Brianne glanced at Christian and bit her bottom lip to keep from laughing. The man looked as if he'd just been in battle with a lion rather than a shooing match with a house cat.

"She doesn't have to find us," D'Artagnan said. "We're right here."

"Lucky us," Brianne said under her breath, and wondered what havoc they had on their agenda for the morning.

Never Alone

Mace spent the day in town alone. First he went to the library, then to the local historical society's office. He ate lunch at one of the restaurants the local fishermen patronized, and used a public phone to make several calls to New Orleans. By the time he returned to LeiMonte, he had gathered quite a bit of information and managed to get answers to several of the questions that had been on his mind since his arrival.

Melanstrup would be pleased, which should have made Mace feel pretty good. Instead he felt lousy.

He drove back to the castle, arriving just as the others were gathering in the parlor for an aperitif. He barely had time to run upstairs and change.

Brianne glanced at him as he entered the parlor. A second later Mrs. Peel's dinner bell summoned them to the dining room.

"May I?" Christian asked, offering Brianne his arm.

A hand at her back pushed her slightly toward Christian.

"Take his arm, Brianne," Aramis ordered softly.

Lizbeth glared at Brianne.

Brianne dug in her heels, resisting Aramis's nudge, and smiled at Christian. "Thank you, Mr. Deuvelle, but I need to talk with Mr. Calder for a moment before dinner."

"Brianne, you are a trial," Aramis said, shaking his head.

"You should talk," she whispered. She moved

to stand beside Mace and stared out at the night beyond the French doors. "Lord, save me from Frenchmen."

Mace retrieved two glasses of wine from the nearby bar and handed her one. His gaze raked over the snug-fitting black silk pants she wore, then he noticed how her white blouse accentuated the fiery hue of her hair. His fingers suddenly ached to plunge into those luxurious strands. He cleared his throat. "Did you really have something to talk to me about, or was that just an excuse?" He offered her his arm.

"He's very nice but . . ." She shrugged and started to slip her arm around his, then paused, nearly holding her breath as she waited for something to topple, crash, careen, or shatter.

The room remained silent.

Brianne didn't know if that meant *they* had decided not to force the issue, or if they'd retired somewhere else to plan their strategy. She prayed it was the former and slipped her arm through Mace's. Instantly she wished she hadn't done so. She'd already been more physically aware of him than she cared to be, but the feel of his arm beneath her hand only intensified that awareness. Her muscles at once tensed and melted. A knot formed in her stomach.

His gaze met hers, and in that instant Brianne knew that if she was ever to be possessed by a man, she wanted it to be this one.

The front door slammed.

Brianne jumped and thoughts of passion shattered.

"Curse the SOBs," Felix snarled loudly, stomping across the foyer. "Dirty-dealing, low-life, belly-crawling snakes."

Brianne tore herself away from Mace and ran into the foyer. "Uncle Felix, what's wrong?"

"Wrong?" He stopped and stared at her.

The other guests had all heard the commotion and rose to gather at the dining-room door.

Mrs. Peel ran into the foyer, a large serving platter clutched in her hands, her attention riveted on Felix.

"I'll tell you what's wrong," he said with a growl, throwing his hat toward the coat tree and jerking his tie loose. "Cummings and those fools he hired to oversee public relations have quit and gone over to Almagamoura, that's what's wrong. Yellow-bellied snakes. Ingrates said they wouldn't stay and work for a company whose owner put an inexperienced relative in charge rather than promote his own vice-presidents."

Brianne felt her face flush, not so much from embarrassment as from anger. Cummings had let her know in no uncertain terms over the last few months that he felt he should have been the one appointed to run St. John Shipping, but she'd never thought he would betray Felix. "Uncle Felix, maybe I should talk to—"

"I'll get the last laugh, though," Felix continued as if she hadn't even spoken. "You just wait. If that SOB Cummings thinks he can pull one over on me, he's mistaken." Crashing his cane onto the floor with each step as if trying to pierce it through the hardwood, Felix stalked into the dining room and took his place at the head of the table.

He looked up as everyone stared at him. "So, what are you all waiting for? Sit!"

Everyone scrambled for a chair.

"Send Porthos after him, that's what I ought to do," Felix muttered.

"At your service, m'sieur," Porthos said, smiling widely as he materialized beside Felix.

Brianne nearly groaned aloud.

"Oh, dinner looks scrumptious," Christian exclaimed as Mrs. Peel placed a platter of deep-fried soft-shelled crabs on the table.

"Eat!" Felix ordered. "And be quiet so I can think."

Brianne stared at her uncle. Well, that was one way of assuring that their guests wouldn't come back or recommend the place.

Over the next half hour Felix continually broke out in growled comments toward his ex–vice-president, which most at the table tried to ignore.

While this was going on, Mace looked at Brianne. "I was thinking of driving into New Orleans tonight," he said softly. "I was hoping you'd come with me."

He was a tourist, a visitor, a man only in

Never Alone

town—at LeiMonte—for a brief vacation. He would be gone in a few days. The Musketeers didn't like him. She really didn't know that much about him—except that she felt as if she'd met him before. All good reasons not to let herself become involved with him, all good reasons not to let this attraction she felt toward him go any further. But it was already too late and Brianne knew it.

A crooked smile lifted one corner of his mouth as he waited for her answer.

"Oh, how fun," Christian exclaimed. "Lizbeth and I could go with you and make it a foursome. Maybe we could even visit a club or two on Bourbon Street. I've heard they're terribly wicked."

Mace and Brianne turned to look at him, startled.

Felix's gaze moved between Mace and Brianne, then settled coldly on Christian. "No."

Startled by his curt outburst, everyone turned to look at the old man.

D'Artagnan suddenly appeared beside Felix and stuck his nose in the old man's face. "What do you mean, no? He should go with Brianne. Look at what an attractive couple they would make." He waved a hand toward Brianne and Christian.

"You must stay here, Mr. Deuvelle," Felix said, studiously ignoring D'Artagnan. "We need to talk."

"What is he doing?" Porthos nearly screamed.

D'Artagnan shrugged and walked away. "Mucking things up, as usual."

Christian looked shocked beyond words and turned to stare at Felix. "Talk? Us?"

"Yes."

Brianne glanced over her shoulder at D'Artagnan and then looked back at Mace. There was no sense tempting fate. "Thank you, Mr. Calder," she said, "but I really do have work—"

"Go," Felix said.

She jerked around to look at her uncle.

"I need some papers from the office, and you can stop by and pick them up."

Brianne frowned. "Trudy can fax them in the morning."

Felix's gaze bored into hers. "I want the originals."

"I can drive in and get them in the morning."

"I want them tonight."

Brianne sighed. She knew when she'd lost a battle, though it would have been nice to know what it had really been all about.

She decided to try one more time. "I could call one of the boys from the mailroom to bring them out."

"They're in my safe," Felix said. "You have to go."

Brianne nodded, though unexpectedly she didn't feel in the least sorry she hadn't won the argument.

An hour later Brianne was sitting beside Mace in the sleek, low sports car he had rented as he drove down LeiMonte's long entry drive.

Porthos suddenly threw himself onto the hood of the car.

Startled, Brianne jumped in her seat and shrieked.

Mace slammed on the brakes and twisted around to look at her. "What?"

Porthos smiled. "You shouldn't be going with him, you know?"

Brianne pressed a hand to her breast, as if to slow the sudden racing of her heart, waved the other at Mace, and inhaled deeply. If the tall Musketeer hadn't already been dead, she knew she would probably have killed him long ago over one or another of his antics.

Mace stared at her. "Are you okay? Why'd you scream?"

"We don't approve of him, Bri," Porthos said, lazing back on the hood and staring up at the sky.

"Why?" Brianne choked out softly.

Mace thought she was echoing his question and remained silent.

"Because he's English," Porthos said. "And"—he remembered the message on the man's little lighted box and frowned—"sneaky. Now, Deuvelle, there's a man." Porthos smiled. "He's cultured, polished, sophisticated, and—"

"French!" Brianne snapped, her temper suddenly getting the better of her.

"French?" Mace echoed, looking confused.

"Well, that certainly does make a difference," Porthos said. "He's also a—"

"Wimp!" Brianne spat.

Mace frowned, fire sparking from his dark eyes. "Excuse me?" he asked.

Porthos looked at her haughtily. "That is not what I was going to say, Bri. I was merely going to mention that he is also handsome."

Brianne briefly closed her eyes, swallowed hard, and took a deep breath in an effort to calm herself. This wasn't happening. She was not having a heated conversation with a ghost while Mace Calder was watching her and obviously thinking she had rocks for brains. She forced a smile to her lips and turned toward him. "Sorry. I was thinking about work, and the solution to something that has been eluding me just popped into my mind."

"Really?" Mace asked, his tone tinged with disbelief. "French wimps?"

She grimaced. "Yes." She put a hand to her cheek and behind it stuck her tongue out at Porthos. "So," she said to Mace, "shall we go on?"

Porthos rolled over and shoved his head through the window. "No."

Mace pulled the gearshift into first and stepped on the gas pedal.

The car shot forward and Porthos flew straight through it, out the back window, and rolled to the ground. Standing, he glared after the car's disappearing taillights, then whipped his wide-brimmed hat from his head and slapped it against his pants to brush himself off. "I knew I didn't like that man."

Turning, he walked toward the house. "D'Artagnan!" he yelled. "Athos! Aramis! We have a war to plan!"

THIRTEEN

Mrs. Peel walked into the library and scanned the bookshelves. The book Felix wanted was on the third shelf from the top. She grabbed the mahogany ladder that was attached to a runner at the top of the shelf and pulled it into place.

She would have asked her husband to get it, but he was still out in the potting shed fiddling with some new concoction of soil for his geraniums. She paused halfway up the ladder and reached for the *Book of the Year, 1972*. It, along with half a dozen other books on the shelf, toppled to the floor with a loud crash.

"Peel," Felix shouted from the study, "you all right?"

Mrs. Peel hurriedly descended the ladder. "Fine," she called back, not wanting him to come into the room and see up her skirt.

She bent to pick up the books. "Oh, my Lordy

me." She gasped, staring at one that had fallen open. Picking it up, she flopped down in a nearby chair and, putting on the glasses that hung from a chain around her neck, stared at the picture that had caught her attention. Long seconds later she shook her head and read the caption under the picture.

Richard Aramis Moret, great-grandson of the famed Musketeer Aramis.

"Oh, my Lordy me," Mrs. Peel whispered again. Getting to her feet, she reached for the phone that sat on a nearby table and quickly dialed her daughter.

"Emily," Mrs. Peel said, "you still doing that genealogy stuff on your computer? Good, I need you to trace someone for me." She looked back at the picture of the man who had been dead for over two hundred years, but looked remarkably like Mace Calder.

"I thought you said you 'needed' to come into town tonight," Brianne said. She kept her gaze averted from Mace's and stared out at the lights of New Orleans in the distance, glistening against the dark sky and reflecting like floating diamonds in the slowly lapping waves of the Mississippi.

Mace leaned one hip against the riverboat's ornate railing and looked at her. "I did."

"Oh?" She felt his nearness, was more aware of him than of any man she'd ever been with, and clutched the railing with both hands. The feelings assailing her were unnerving and exciting, but she wasn't certain whether she should damn them or welcome them.

"I felt the need to take a riverboat ride under the stars with a beautiful woman by my side."

He moved closer and slipped an arm around her waist.

The sensations sweeping through her caused her hands to tremble and created a hollow feeling deep within her chest. "And are your needs satisfied now?" she asked softly.

"Not quite."

She turned to him then and an ache of wanting erupted in Mace like an assaulting blow. It flashed through his body, burned in his blood, scorched his flesh, and settled in a knot of need within his loins.

Brianne St. John was the essence of his every desire, and he wanted her . . . but not because of the deal. He wanted her because he needed her, because she'd touched something in him he thought no one could reach.

As she looked up into his eyes an invisible net of passion wove its threads through the air around them, then settled upon their souls.

"Brianne," Mace whispered, and dragged her into his arms. He crushed her body to his, needing to feel her against him, needing to hold her, touch her, kiss her.

She reached up to touch his face, cupping his cheek in her hand, and he knew he was lost, the featherlight touch like a seductive caress to his scarred soul. It silently, tenderly seized him, pulled him over the edge of need, and banished all doubt and fear from his thoughts.

Brianne gazed directly into his eyes as his head lowered toward hers. She knew *they* could be there, watching, waiting to interrupt, but she didn't care. At this moment all she wanted, all she could think about was her desire to be kissed by Mace, held by him, loved by him.

In spite of the kisses they had shared before, this time was different. The heat of his body enveloped her, the savage virility of his lips robbed her of breath, and something deep within her whispered that dreams really did come true.

His strength and passion became hers.

She slipped her tongue between his lips, her arms around his neck, and pressed her body to his length. Need and want made her brazen, chased away the inhibitions of inexperience, banished the doubt caused by the unknown, and the hesitation born of the earlier flashes of déjà vu.

"Brianne, Brianne," Mace said between gasps, his lips moving from hers to travel over her cheek, along the line of her jaw, down the slope of her neck. "I want you," he whispered against her throat. The anguish of need and desire turned his voice as dark and dusky as the night. "I've waited forever for you"—he claimed her lips again, then tore them away—"and I don't think I can wait any longer."

She clung to him, her fingers entwining within the black tendrils of his hair, feeling the silky strands slip over her flesh. Longing burned within her body, need gripped her in a delirium of desire. Whatever else was to happen in her life, she knew that being with Mace, loving him now, was right. It was what she wanted. He was what she wanted.

A tiny voice in the back of Mace's mind tried to call out to him, to warn him. These feelings were too dangerous. He'd come there for business. He was losing control. He'd be sorry. But he refused to listen. All he wanted was to be with Brianne St. John, to feel her naked body, hot and covered by a sheen of passion, pressed to his, to join his need with hers and love her.

Her lips reclaimed his, ravishing his mouth as he had done to hers.

Hot, deep, burning hunger flared within Mace as she gave him everything she had to offer, and demanded the same from him. Need, more intense than anything he'd ever felt in his life, ripped through him, tore at his gut, and threatened to bring him to his knees.

The whistle of the riverboat suddenly blared, signaling its return to the docks.

Brianne pulled away, then looked up into Mace's eyes. "I have a place in town," she said quietly.

He held his breath, fear that he had merely dreamed her words hovering about his mind.

She slipped her hand into his.

"Are you sure?" Mace said. It was a question he had never asked a woman before, but he knew, unexplainably, that he had to ask it of her.

Brianne smiled and urged him toward the front of the boat as it turned toward the wharf.

They left the car where it was and walked the two blocks to Brianne's apartment in the French Quarter, where, she'd explained on the way, she often stayed when she worked late at the office.

Whatever the direction they walked, Mace was oblivious, just as he was when they entered the apartment. It could have been decorated in alligator hides and swamp grass or priceless fifteenth-century antiques for all he knew. All he was aware of, all he wanted to be aware of, was Brianne.

The entry door no sooner closed behind them than Mace dragged her back into his arms. Everything about her was soft and warm, her body pliant and supple pressed against his. The grace of her curves filled the hard planes of his body as they melded into each other, leaving no space for light or air between them. Releasing the agonized growl of need that had been building in his throat since they'd kissed on the riverboat, his lips crashed down on hers. His tongue plunged into her mouth to dance a duel with her own, and his hand moved to cup her breast. The loneliness, need, and urgency of long pent-up and denied emotions raged through him on a tidal wave of desire.

Brianne arched against him, the yearning ache within her to be touched everywhere by him almost more than she could bear. It pervaded and conquered her every sense, sending all thought of anything but Mace Calder from her mind.

His thumb flicked over the pebbled peak of her nipple, stoking her hunger.

Brianne had never felt such fire. She was being consumed by it, and instinctively knew the only salve was him. The fire spread through her body, turned her languid in his arms, and fueled the hunger of her desires.

Moving instinctively, her hands slid under his jacket and pulled at the buttons on his shirt.

The touch of her fingers burned into his flesh as they moved sensuously over his chest, teasing his passion, tantalizing his desires.

Within minutes their clothes lay on the floor at their feet and their naked bodies were pressed together.

"Brianne," Mace whispered, his lips moving down her throat.

She shivered in his arms and snuggled closer. A soft sigh of pleasure slipped from her lips as his hand slid down her side and over her hip.

The sound tore at him, seized hold of something deep within him, and refused to let go. He wanted her, needed her, more than he had ever wanted or needed anything in his life, and if having her, if giving in to these feelings swirling within him meant losing the deal, losing Melanstrup's business, then he was already lost.

Mace bent and, swinging an arm around the

back of her legs, swept her into his arms. Cradling her against his chest, his lips continuing to travel in tender, nipping forays down the long column of her neck, he carried her into the bedroom. Beside the bed he paused, though it took every ounce of strength and willpower he possessed. "If you're not sure," he said huskily, each word ripped from his throat with agonized effort, "if you want me to stop, tell me now." He laid her on the bed but didn't join her. "Because later it will be too late."

Moonlight flowing through the bedroom's windows bathed him in a soft amber haze. A flush of warmth suddenly burned Brianne's cheeks, then rushed through her entire body as her traitorous gaze dropped away from his and moved wantonly over his naked body.

Everything about him was magnificent. His shoulders were broad, his arms well-honed lengths of muscle, and his chest a hard wall of sinew. Everything about him screamed strength and power, yet she knew firsthand that he was also gentle. Her eyes moved from the corrugated landscape of his ribs downward, over the taut line of his stomach, and followed a thin line of silken black hairs to the dense forest that surrounded the rigid evidence of his arousal.

She reached up for him, took his hand in hers, and pulled him down to the bed. Physical need pierced his body like a jolt of lightning as her hands slid over him intimately. His lips moved down the length of her throat, then surrounded one nipple as his hand caressed the other.

Brianne writhed against him, seized by sensations of passion awakening in her body for the first time. Shivers of pleasure rippled over the surface of her skin as his hands wrought exquisite torture everywhere they touched.

Mace felt as if his body were about to explode from the want swirling within him.

Brianne twisted in response to the caress of his hands, arched upward in answer to the taunting touch of his tongue to her breast, and moaned when his fingers slipped between her thighs.

Nothing in life had prepared her for Mace Calder and the feelings he was igniting within her, and yet she knew he was exactly the man she had been waiting for. He was her other self, he was the man who would complete the circle of her soul, the only man she would ever truly love as completely as a woman loves a man.

He touched her everywhere.

She responded in kind.

He felt his hunger for her deepen.

She gasped at the pleasure his touch ignited within her.

Featherlight caresses teased her mind and body, burned her skin, seared into her soul, and whispered that she was his forever.

She cried out for him.

He knew he could wait no longer.

He rose above her. "Brianne?" he said huskily, looking down at her.

She looked up at him. Tears filled her eyes. "Love me," she whispered, and reached for him, wrapping a leg around his, pulling him closer, needing him with every cell, every ounce of her being.

His lips took hers, tender and savage, claiming and surrendering as he plunged inside of her.

A thousand flames of passion burst within him as she wrapped her warmth around him and pulled him into her. An inferno of need, delicious and tormenting, deep and gnawing, erupted within her. Whatever rational thought still lingered in her mind was instantly banished.

He felt her hunger move through her body like a shiver on the wind, inciting, stoking his own.

She cried out his name.

Mace covered her lips with his.

Brianne reveled in the melding of their bodies, exulting in his possession of her and her possession of him. Each movement created a new flame of passion, fusing their flesh.

Each thrust of his body was fiercer than the last, each caress more demanding, each kiss more ruthless and pillaging, and she surrendered wholly—willingly—eagerly.

They moved as one, with no inhibitions, no hesitations, their only emotion desire.

Her hands roamed his body, sliding over the corded muscles of his shoulders, delving into the hollow of his spine, rippling over the terrace of his ribs, the curve of his buttocks.

A groan of pleasure broke from Mace's mouth, echoing into hers.

Suddenly every sensation in Brianne's body changed, crashed, and exploded. Fire raced through her veins, yearning swept through her loins, and the most incredible sense of fulfillment washed over her as wave after wave of rapture erupted from deep within her being.

Mace clutched her to him and heard his name rip from her lips over and over, a desperation of feeling in her tone that touched him like nothing in the world had ever done before. She trembled within the throes of climax, her arms grasping his shoulders, holding to him as if she'd never let him go.

Passion, need, want, and hunger erupted with him, hot, wild, violently delicious sensations that tore through him mercilessly, conquering every ounce of his strength with its force. The breath in his lungs stalled, the beat of his heart paused, and time stopped.

At that moment, as if nothing in his life that had come before it mattered, or even truly existed, Mace suddenly knew that he wanted Brianne in all of his tomorrows. Without his even knowing how it had happened, or when it had happened, she had made him crave what he'd been convinced he would never want.

Long moments later he had still not released

her from the circle of his arms. He held her to him as his breath returned to normal, as his heart slowed its frantic beat, and the fires of passion smoldered quietly, momentarily satiated.

What they had just done would change everything. He knew that, yet he still didn't care. Maybe later, in the cold light of day, he would care. Maybe he would even regret that it had happened, but not now.

Brianne lay quietly cradled in his arms, feeling totally content for the first time in her life. She trailed her hand down the hard length of his arm, allowed her fingers to delve within the small hollow in the center of his chest, then start a slow, deliberate, and tantalizing trek downward.

"That could be dangerous," Mace said, his voice ragged.

She smiled wickedly. "You're not dangerous."

He rolled over and pinned her to the bed with his body. "You think not?" The challenge in his tone was belied by the spark of desire dancing within his eyes.

"No."

His mouth captured hers, and within seconds Brianne was being taught just how deliciously dangerous Mace Calder could be.

FOURTEEN

With a trembling hand, Athos turned the final page of the journal his ex-wife had written so many years before. Ignoring the gnawing ache in his chest, he continued to read the words that were so fraught with feeling.

> *I have written all of this into a journal, thinking that, perhaps, if my most personal and private thoughts and memories were transferred to paper, they would forever leave my mind and I might find some semblance of peace.*
>
> *For so long I buried my true feelings and only thought of exacting revenge. However, the past years, in which I have betrayed and lied so many more times, all to benefit myself, have taught me that he was right, and I was the foolish one for thinking it could be any other way in the end.*

As Charlotte Backson, Comtesse de la Fère, I had everything I ever dreamed of, including a love so deep and desperate, my heart ached whenever he was away from me. My lies destroyed it all.

Even though my betrayal and lies, and his soul-reaching sense of honor forced him to reject our love and me, I love him still . . . and always will. He was the man of my dreams, the hero of my heart, the love of my soul.

Yet I hurt him beyond belief.

I know now that all I have accomplished by writing my memories within these pages is to relive them rather than forget them. It was a foolish thought. Tonight, after Count Corprovenue's soiree, I shall return home and add this journal to the flames burning within the grate of my bedchamber's fireplace.

Athos blinked away the moisture that had gathered in his eyes as he'd read the last page.

A soft groan of despair slipped from his lips as memory after memory moved slowly through his mind. Finally, unable to look at her picture any longer, he turned away and walked to the windows of her room.

Grief hung on his shoulders like a mantle of steel, heavy and cold. He stared out into the night, seeing but not seeing, his mind's eye traveling back over the years once more.

She had loved him. He had loved her. Nevertheless, they had betrayed each other . . . and in the end they had destroyed each other.

Porthos appeared on the lawn beneath the window where Athos stood.

"Athos, come down," he called. "Brianne hasn't come home and we must decide what to do."

The blond Musketeer stared down at his friend and struggled to put his thoughts of the past aside. Nodding finally, he turned from the window and picked up the journal. They had more important things to do now than try to sabotage the burgeoning relationship between Brianne and Mace Calder.

The others were waiting for him in the parlor.

"He's looking for the box," Athos said, striding into the room.

D'Artagnan stared at him. "What?"

Athos tossed Charlotte's journal onto the table before the other three Musketeers. "Deuvelle—he's looking for our box."

Aramis picked up the journal, flipped through it, then looked up at Athos. "It says that in here?"

"No. What it says in there is that we buried a treasure here."

"How did she know?" Aramis asked. He looked up at Athos. There was question in his eyes rather than accusation.

Athos shrugged. "She was Richelieu's spy. She had her ways of finding things out."

D'Artagnan looked at the others. "So Deuvelle

is looking for a treasure." He shrugged. "Let him look. He'll never find anything."

"Maybe we should just keep an eye on him to make certain of that," Porthos said, whipping out his sword. "I'll volunteer to go first." He smiled wickedly. "Since I have one of my days coming up."

"I should have called home last night," Brianne said, looking across the table at Mace, "and told them . . . something."

A waiter appeared and refilled her coffee cup.

Mace waited until he'd left. "You should have remained a bit longer in bed this morning."

The look in his eyes was so sinfully seductive, Brianne felt a warm flush spread rapidly through her body.

He reached across the table and touched her cheek. "I like it when you do that," he said softly, huskily.

She cocked her head. "Do what?"

"Blush." He smiled.

Brianne's blush burned deeper.

"I need to stop by the office and pick up those papers for Felix," she said.

Her reference to her work steered Mace's thoughts in a direction he'd been trying to avoid. He glanced at his watch. Since he hadn't called Melanstrup the night before, the man had probably sent him about five hundred E-mails by now, demanding to hear a progress report.

With that thought, his head declared an immediate war against his heart. He couldn't go through with Melanstrup's deal and continue a relationship with Brianne. But he'd worked too hard to get where he was to give it all up for a woman. Especially since, in his experience, such a sacrifice was never justified. Anyway, what he was feeling, what he'd felt the previous night, was nothing more than an attraction for an especially alluring woman. Maybe a little more intense than ever before, but it would pass. It always did, one way or another.

"Where are you?" Brianne asked, breaking into his thoughts.

Mace started. "What?"

"You seemed a million miles away. I just wondered where."

He smiled. "Remembering last night," he said softly, "and wishing it hadn't ended."

She blushed again.

Twenty minutes later they pulled Mace's car to the curb in front of St. John Shipping and walked into Brianne's office.

Trudy gave Mace the once-over, cocked a brow at Brianne, and smiled. She handed Brianne a stack of messages. "Broadelay's lawyer called. Felix has been trying to reach you, Cummings has made surreptitious calls to three people in the company this

Never Alone

morning, and Randall Dreay has been making noise about leaving if he isn't appointed to the PR director's job."

"Terrific," Brianne said. "Any good news?"

Trudy smiled and glanced at Mace again. "Not on my end. How about yours?"

Brianne sighed. "I have to get some papers from the safe. Call me at LeiMonte if you need to."

Mace followed her into the office Felix still kept at the company headquarters, and leaned a hip against the huge cherrywood desk that dominated the room while she opened the safe.

He'd nearly choked on his own breath when her secretary had mentioned that Broadelay's lawyer had called Brianne. Now he was wondering why, since Broadelay had been in negotiations with Melanstrup when Mace had left San Francisco a few days earlier.

He looked back at Brianne as she stood by the safe examining several documents. Thinking there was something between them was ludicrous. The last thing in the world he wanted was a relationship, especially a serious one, and he had the distinct feeling that that was the only kind Brianne St. John was interested in. He had too much riding on this deal to throw it away because he'd let desire get the better of reason.

As if to argue the point, his body hardened as Brianne turned to him and his gaze swept over her.

"Okay, I've got what Felix wanted." She smiled

as she tucked the papers into her purse. "Shall we go?"

Mace pushed away from the desk and closed the space between them.

Brianne looked up at him, puzzled.

He slid her purse from her shoulder and let it drop to the floor, then pulled her into his arms.

"Mace?"

He was putting everything he had, everything he'd accomplished on the line. What he was about to do was wrong, and she would end up hurt, but he had to prove to himself, to his heart, that it did not rule him, could never rule him.

His lips crashed down on hers as if he were a conqueror claiming his victim.

Brianne felt the savage demand of his kiss, the desperate strength of his embrace, and leaned into him, breathless from his sudden assault.

Mace's thoughts spun and the world tilted on him. Suddenly he couldn't stop the kiss he'd started only to prove to himself that he didn't need it. His soul could desert him, the world as he knew it could disappear, and he knew he couldn't stop, wouldn't care. His desire for Brianne was immeasurable and undeniable.

"Mace, we need to . . ."

His lips brushed across hers, igniting flame.

". . . stop . . . can't . . ."

His mouth returned to claim hers, caressing each corner with his tongue.

Never Alone

"Not here," she said, breathing deeply, nearly moaning out her pleasure.

"Yes, here," he said, his lips moving over her throat and teasing the flesh of her neck.

Brianne's arms encircled his shoulders. She had no control over herself with him, no will to stop him. She wanted him, had wanted him from the moment they'd met, and would always want him.

"You're wicked," she whispered against his neck, nipping his flesh with her teeth.

"You make me that way," he said with a groan. His lips reclaimed hers, a heated demand that was more assault than caress. His tongue moved around hers, dancing, dueling, igniting fire throughout her mouth.

Need flowed through him, invading every part of his body and leaving him hungry with desire. The need to make love to her again overwhelmed him.

His hands moved to her breasts.

Brianne gasped sharply at the intimate touch as her body arched toward his, silently begging him not to stop. Burning waves of need seared through her.

FIFTEEN

"Oh, Miss St. John had to go into the city," Mrs. Peel replied to Christian's inquiry as he and Lizbeth stepped into the foyer.

Christian smiled. This was exactly what he'd been waiting for. Mace Calder's red sports car hadn't been in the drive, which meant both he and Brianne were away from the house. But he had to hurry. The Tower Room and Brianne's bedchamber were the only rooms so far, besides the kitchen, that he had been unable to search, and this might be his only opportunity.

He hurriedly extricated himself from the arm Lizbeth had possessively wrapped around him. "I really must go to my room for a minute," he said, and made for the stairs.

The same moment he stepped into the Tower Room, Mace's computer beeped, drawing Christian's attention. He moved to the desk and looked down at the screen. A list of at least a dozen E-mail messages covered the screen, all from the same person, and all sent since the previous night.

Curiosity got the better of him. Christian moved the cursor to the first message and pressed "read." A moment later excitement flowed through his blood. He went on to the next message, and then the next. He was reading the ninth when he heard the sound of tires rolling over the crushed-shell drive. Jumping up, he ran to the window and looked out.

Mace's sports car pulled up before the house.

"Damn," Christian cursed. He returned to the computer and closed down the letter he'd been reading, then dashed for the door. He hadn't had time to search the room, but it didn't matter now. After he told Brianne what he'd learned, Mace Calder would be about as welcome at LeiMonte as a horde of rats.

Christian arrived at the bottom of the grand staircase at the same moment Brianne opened the front door and walked into the foyer.

"Good afternoon, Christian," she said.

He moved to stand before her and took her hand in his, making certain to keep a grave look on his face and his gaze averted from Mace's. "May I speak to you privately?" he asked softly.

Brianne frowned. "Is something wrong?"

He nodded solemnly. "I'm afraid so."

"With your accommodations?"

He shook his head. "No, but please, this is a matter of the utmost importance."

She looked back at Mace. "I'm sorry, I'll . . ."

Mace looked at the other man sharply, his dark gaze boring into him, then turned to Brianne and shook his head. "I have a few things to do anyway. Calls to make. I'll see you at dinner." He touched her arm as he passed, a caress that was not a caress, and mounted the stairs.

Christian watched until he was out of sight, then turned back to Brianne.

"Come into the study," she said, and walked toward its open door.

Christian followed and closed the door behind him.

Brianne felt a moment's temper as he did so. She moved around her desk to put it between herself and the Frenchman. She didn't know what it was about Christian Deuvelle that seemed to aggravate her. His constant efforts at flirtation were an annoyance, that was certain, but there was something more she couldn't put her finger on. "So, what is the problem?" she asked coolly.

"Mr. Calder . . ."

"Mace?" Brianne said, startled.

Christian nodded gravely. "I thought you should know that Mr. Calder is not who he pretends to be."

Brianne sat down.

Christian took one of the wing chairs opposite her. "He is a corporate raider, and his client, Donald J. Melanstrup, is interested in initiating a hostile takeover of St. John Shipping."

Brianne shot to her feet. Shock and disbelief had drained the blood from her face. "Where did you hear that?"

But as soon as she asked the question, she knew it was irrelevant, because she suddenly knew exactly why she'd thought she had seen Mace somewhere before, ever since he'd arrived at LeiMonte. Nine months earlier a wealthy California man had engaged in a hostile takeover of the LaRue hotel chain in the French Quarter, and he'd won, with the aid of a corporate raider named James M. Calder.

Christian shook his head. "I'm sorry, my sources are confidential, but I thought you should know." He stood. "Again, I am truly sorry, since it seems that you and Mr. Calder—"

"There is nothing between me and Mace Calder," Brianne snapped. She fought for composure, took a deep breath, and clenched her hands into fists. "Thank you for telling me this, Christian," she said softly. "Now, if you'll excuse me, I have some calls to make."

He nodded and left the room, smiling smugly as he closed the door behind him.

Mace stood in the doorway to the kitchen, where he'd gone for a cool drink, and watched the Frenchman disappear into the parlor. He didn't like the smug look he'd glimpsed on the man's face.

Brianne collapsed back into her chair and stared

at nothing. A corporate raider, and his goal was to take over St. John Shipping. He was there to spy on them.

"Fool," she whispered sharply. Tears filled her eyes. How could she have been such a fool? He'd used her, made her think he cared for her, and all he'd wanted was information that would help his client succeed in taking over Felix's company.

Blinking back her tears as another thought struck, Brianne jumped to her feet again and ran into the foyer. She grabbed the purse she'd left on the small table by the door and jerked it open. Everything looked as it should. She grabbed the papers she'd taken from the office safe, shuffled through them quickly, then sighed in relief to see that they were all there.

But had he seen them? Did it matter?

She walked back into her office, slid the papers into a drawer of the desk, and locked it, then sat back and stared across the room. Who was Donald J. Melanstrup? Brianne picked up the phone and dialed the company's attorney.

Mace stared at his computer screen. A deep frown pulled at his brow as he sat back in his chair. Someone had been in his room and read his E-mail. He reached for the cursor button again and scrolled down the list of incoming messages. Fourteen messages in total, and nine flaps of the small envelope icons beside the name of each message were open, which meant nine out of the fourteen new messages had been read. Mace thumped a fist onto the desk. He hadn't read any of them until now, and he certainly didn't believe the ghost of some long-dead Musketeer had been playing around with his computer.

He got up and walked around the room, probing with his eyes, trying to discern if anything had been taken, or even moved.

A moment later he decided nothing else had been touched. He looked back at the computer. Only two people in this house had a reason to want a look at his computer: Felix and Brianne. She was out because she had been with him.

That left the old man. Several comments he'd overheard led Mace to believe that Felix was computer illiterate.

But why would they suspect him? He hadn't done anything to give himself away. Unless they'd recognized him and figured out why he was there.

Mace turned to stand before the window, looking out at the vast landscape surrounding the castle.

But how could they have found out who he was? Why he was at LeiMonte? He hadn't even used his first name. People in the business knew him as James, not Mace, or even Mason. And it wasn't as if his picture was in the newspapers very often. Hell, only once that he even remembered, and that had been because he'd been engaged to

Jaclyn, not because the society-page writers had been interested in him.

Anxiety refused to let him stand still. He began to pace the room.

If she had known why he was at LeiMonte, she would never have gone out with him. Mace stopped. "She wouldn't have made love with me," he mumbled.

Porthos, having just walked through the door and into the room, stopped dead in his tracks at hearing Mace's comment. "Make love?" he gasped, his goatee-covered chin dropping nearly to his chest. Spinning on his heel, he barreled out of the room, bellowing for the other Musketeers as he stomped down the spiral stairway.

Brianne heard Porthos's rumbles echoing through the house and stiffened.

"Musketeers!" Porthos roared. "Musketeers!"

Brianne regathered her senses and control over her body, jumped to her feet, and ran to the door. Flinging it open, she looked up the stairs.

The sound of booted feet running across hardwood floors and swords being drawn from their metal sheaths echoed throughout the house.

"Oh, God," she said in alarm. In all her years at LeiMonte she had never heard anything like this. It sounded as if they were charging about in preparation to defend the place against marauders. She hurried to the bottom of the staircase, but the moment she reached it, the sounds disappeared and the house fell quiet again. She waited, but nothing happened, and she felt no sense of their presence nearby. "What's wrong?" she asked aloud, and looked around, waiting.

Silence was her only answer.

"Where are you? What's going on?"

Again, nothing.

She walked back into her study.

The phone on her desk rang, nearly sending Brianne through the ceiling. She ran across the room and grabbed the receiver. "Yes?"

"Miss St. John?"

"Yes."

"This is Andrew Zachary."

"Oh, yes, Andrew," Brianne said. It was the company attorney.

"I have that information you wanted on Melanstrup and Calder."

Brianne braced herself.

"Calder is a corporate raider."

Athos suddenly took form beside the fireplace, a worried look on his face.

"Mace is a corporate raider," Brianne repeated, as if trying to convince herself of what she'd just heard.

"Yes, though professionally he goes by the name James M. Calder. He's one of the best, Brianne."

Athos let his form disappear so she wouldn't see

him and moved to stand beside her, cocking an ear to hear her conversation.

"His clients are varied, but include some of the wealthiest and most powerful men in the country. His techniques have been known to be a bit . . . questionable, but always successful."

"Terrific," Brianne muttered.

"Melanstrup is a wealthy entrepreneur in San Francisco. Got his start by buying an old trucking company whose owner was sick and unable to keep it going. Built it up and went on to acquire several more, buying up the owners' debts and then foreclosing on them. Then he got into the import/export business the same way. Now he wants into shipping. He's hired Calder to help him with a couple of deals in the past, and obviously he's hired him for this one."

"He's targeted a takeover of St. John's rather than buying or establishing his own line," Brianne said, irritation clear in her voice.

"Yes. It seems to be his preferred way of doing business."

"Well, this time he's not going to get his way," Brianne snapped. She hung up and immediately called the office. An hour and several lengthy discussions later she felt confident her staff knew what to do to prepare to fight a takeover.

A knock on the door drew her attention. "What?" she snapped, still too angry even to attempt a semblance of politeness.

Mace opened the door and stepped into the room. "Is it safe in here?" he asked, smiling.

Brianne stood and walked around the desk. "For you, no."

He paused, halfway into the room, suddenly realizing that her anger was directed at him. "What's wrong?"

"When were you going to tell me the truth, Mr. Calder? Upon your departure?"

Mrs. Peel was on her way through the foyer to get the front door for Felix, who'd just returned from visiting a neighbor. She paused, looked into the study, then hurried on to the door.

Brianne's eyes blazed with fury as she stared at Mace. "Or were you going to wait until you got back to San Francisco and started your wheels of greed rolling?"

Felix stepped into the room quietly but remained by the door, Mrs. Peel just behind him.

"Or maybe," Brianne went on coldly, not even aware of her uncle's appearance, "you weren't going to tell me at all. Maybe I was supposed to figure it out on my own when Donald J. Melanstrup took over St. John Shipping."

Mace felt his body go cold, the blood in his veins cease to flow, and a giant-size lump of lead fall to the pit of his stomach.

"You're very good at what you do, Mr. Calder," Brianne went on icily. "I never would have thought of seduction as a tool of business, but maybe that's what separates the boys from the girls."

The truth of his feelings crashed down on him. Everything he wanted was standing in front of him, rejecting him, denouncing him. He couldn't let that happen. He couldn't lose her. "Brianne, no, I . . ." He took a step toward her.

She backed away quickly. "Don't touch me!"

"Brianne, you've got to listen, I—"

"I want you out of LeiMonte, Mr. Calder. Pack your bags and leave. Now."

Mace stared at her. If he left, he knew he'd never see her again. She would refuse to take his phone calls and reject any attempt he made to see her, talk to her. Something cold and destructive sliced through his heart. He couldn't let this happen. He loved her.

The thought stunned him. He looked at her for a long moment and knew then that if he walked away now, he would lose, forever, the only woman he'd ever really loved. Mace stiffened. "I have a reservation, Brianne. I'm not leaving."

She glared at him, hatred and anger swirling in the blue depths of her eyes. "You're no longer welcome in my home."

He shrugged. "The Pilgrimage Society took my reservation, which entitles me to a room here, and my stay is not concluded. Sorry, but I'm not leaving."

On his way to the parlor, Christian had paused on the stairs at the sounds of Brianne and Mace arguing. Upon hearing her order Calder to leave LeiMonte, he had nearly danced with glee. Hearing Mace refuse, however, had sent him spiraling into the depths of despair. If Mace wouldn't leave, Christian couldn't search the Tower Room, and he was scheduled to return to France in two days' time.

Turning on his heel, he hurried back upstairs and raced toward the staircase leading to the Tower Room. If they argued long enough, perhaps he could search the room thoroughly now. If Mace returned and caught him, he'd just say . . . he'd say . . . Oh, posh, Christian swore silently. He'd think of something to say.

He moved quickly to the bookcases that lined the east wall. Minutes later he ran his hands over the posts of the tall canopy bed, then pulled out each drawer of the bureau and looked behind it for hidden compartments.

An elaborately decorated cherry- and lemonwood window seat was set into the south-side wall. Christian dropped to his knees and began feeling around its delicate carved sides.

Serendipity, whose "nest" was only inches from one side of the window seat, glared at him. A low growl emanated from deep in her chest.

Christian jumped, then stared at the cat, not having even realized she was there.

Six little kittens were pressed to her stomach, suckling contentedly.

"Shoo!" Christian said, flapping his hands to get her to rise and move away. "Shoo, shoo, shoo."

Serendipity's lips curled back and she hissed angrily, then swatted at one of Christian's hands.

"Ow," he shrieked as one of the cat's claws sliced through his skin. Christian fell to his rear, then scrambled backward, scooting across the floor on hands and feet like an awkward crab.

Running into the bed, he stopped, grabbed a pillow, and tossed it at the cat.

She snarled loudly and leaped at him.

Christian screamed as the cat landed on his chest.

SIXTEEN

Athos's temper flared as he looked past Brianne at Mace Calder. Love betrayed was the cruelest of all life's sorrows, and if there was anything he could do about it, he would not let Brianne feel its pangs without exacting some revenge.

Ripping off one of his gauntlets, Athos strode across the room toward Mace.

Brianne suddenly felt his presence. "No," she said quickly.

Athos slapped Mace across the face with the glove.

Mace's head jerked to the left as something he couldn't see struck his cheek. "What the . . . ?" He raised a hand to his face, touching the flesh of his stinging cheek. Startled, he glared toward Brianne, realized she was too far away to have slapped him, then scoured the room with his gaze.

Nothing. No one.

He looked back at Brianne. She was staring at him, seemingly apprehensive now. Mace looked around the room again. Could she have been telling the truth? Could the story that LeiMonte was haunted by the Musketeers be true?

Suddenly the outline of a man began to take shape in front of him.

Mace stared at the ethereal figure, like a shadow on the air that was slowly, steadily taking form before his eyes. Translucence slowly turned to solidity, the filmy whiteness of the figure to color.

"Oh, no," he muttered, and shook his head. "This isn't happening."

"Ah, but it is," Athos said, glowering at him. Spinning on his heel, he walked to the swords that hung, one crossed over the other, on the wall near the fireplace. He ripped one from its moorings, then turned and threw it to Mace, hilt first. *"Aux armes,"* he declared.

Mace caught the sword, barely, then stared at Athos.

Suddenly D'Artagnan, Porthos, and Aramis appeared behind Athos.

Mace squeezed his eyes shut and shook his head. Whatever was happening wasn't real. He was having a delusion. Imagining it. He opened his eyes and then looked again. They were still there. Four Musketeers.

Athos approached, sword drawn and raised. *"En garde."*

Mace looked at the Musketeer whose blond

hair hung to his shoulders. Athos flipped the front of his blue cloak over one shoulder, momentarily obscuring the silver fleur-de-lis sewn onto the cloak's breast.

Mace shook his head. "No. This isn't really happening. You're not there."

A smile broke through Athos's dark blond mustache and goatee.

"This isn't real," Mace said again.

Athos's sword sliced the air, and its tip ripped through the front of Mace's shirt.

Brianne stood frozen, not even daring to believe the scene that was unfolding before her.

Mace looked from his shirt to the Musketeer, eyes wide in shock. This was impossible. Wasn't it?

"*En garde*," Athos said again, and raised his sword in readiness.

"No. This isn't . . . you're not there. I'm not fighting."

"Then prepare to die." Athos's sword swooped through the air.

Mace hurriedly raised his own weapon to deflect the silver blade. "This is crazy!"

"This is honor," Athos countered.

"*Bon! Bon!*" Porthos shouted.

Athos lunged.

"Yes!" Felix whispered, enthralled by the sight.

Calling on the long-unused fencing skills he'd learned in college, Mace barely deflected the Musketeer's sword away from his chest.

D'Artagnan heard Serendipity's screech. He

looked toward the stairs. "I think we're needed elsewhere," he said to Porthos and Aramis.

The three instantly disappeared.

Athos jumped to a table, leaped to the floor, and lunged again.

Mace parried.

"Stop," Brianne shouted. The word passed her lips as little more than a gasping whisper.

At that moment the telephone rang.

Mrs. Peel ran across the foyer and grabbed the receiver from its cradle.

"Mama," Mrs. Peel's daughter said, "you were right. He's Aramis's great-grandson nine times removed, on his mother's side."

"Oh, Lordy," Mrs. Peel muttered. "I knew it. I just knew it."

D'Artagnan knelt down before Serendipity. "What is it, *ma petite*?" he said softly. He picked up one of the cat's front paws and noticed the trace of blood on her claw, then stood, frowning with displeasure. "Where is that blasted Frenchman?"

The others shrugged.

"Probably still searching for the treasure," Aramis said. "It seems to be all the man wants to do."

"He's not going to give up," Porthos snapped.

"It could be quite valuable after all this time, D'Artagnan," Aramis said. "A museum piece."

D'Artagnan nodded. "My thoughts exactly.

Never Alone

And I have a feeling that if he finds it, he won't tell Brianne."

"But if he doesn't, we may never get rid of him," Aramis said. "And I have to tell you, I don't really like him. He's too sneaky."

"You'd rather she ended up with the one downstairs?" Porthos exclaimed, seemingly aghast at the idea.

Aramis glared at him. "She loves the one downstairs."

Porthos grumbled incoherently.

"Aramis is right," D'Artagnan said. "We may have preferred she marry a Frenchman, but her heart went elsewhere, and I have to confess, I'm not that fond of Deuvelle myself. Wouldn't be surprised to discover he was descended from the de Médicis."

"So, what do we do?" Porthos demanded.

"Well," Aramis replied, "if we help him find the box, we can tell Brianne before he leaves and she can get it back."

D'Artagnan nodded. "Yes. Good."

They walked into Brianne's room to find Christian standing on a chest examining the ceiling molding.

"The man is an idiot," Porthos spat.

"But a persistent one," Aramis added.

"Porthos," D'Artagnan said, "Athos is busy at the moment, but isn't this one of your days?"

Porthos's lips curled in a grin that was no less wicked than the gleam that sparked in his eyes.

"Oui, mon ami. Tu as raison." He walked to where Christian stood and began rocking the trunk.

Christian screeched, grabbed at the wall, and jumped down, turning to look at the trunk, which suddenly seemed to be alive.

"Now try directing him to the right spot," D'Artagnan said.

Porthos created a whirlwind, toppled a lamp, and finally, in desperation and frustration, grabbed Christian's shirtfront and literally dragged him toward the elegantly scrolled white-marble-and-oak-fronted fireplace.

Christian trembled, muttered to himself, and looked around, obviously terror-stricken. "Who . . . who's here?" he stammered, seconds later.

"This is hopeless," Aramis said.

"Try again," D'Artagnan urged.

Porthos grabbed Christian's shirtsleeve and directed the man's arm toward the fireplace mantel.

Christian gasped loudly and jerked his hand back, then scooted away from the fireplace, his gaze darting wildly around the room.

Aramis chuckled softly. "I haven't seen anyone this frightened since we faced off with Richelieu's last standing guard."

"And he has the audacity to call himself a Frenchman," Porthos spat.

"The cat," D'Artagnan said.

The two Musketeers spun to look at him. "What?" they said in unison.

"The cat. She can show him." D'Artagnan zipped back to the Tower Room. A moment later he was standing in the hall outside of Brianne's door. "Porthos," he called. "Open the door."

Porthos frowned. "Why?"

"Just do it," D'Artagnan ordered.

Porthos walked across the room and opened the door.

Serendipity pranced into the room ahead of D'Artagnan.

The Musketeers watched her walk calmly over to Christian and rub her body against his legs.

"I thought she hated him," Aramis said.

"She does," D'Artagnan said.

Aramis turned. "Then how did you get her to do that?"

D'Artagnan smiled. "Animals like me. And she loves Brianne."

Christian stared at the cat as if expecting her to turn into Godzilla and pounce on him.

"This isn't working," Porthos grumbled. "The man is afraid of her too."

"Wait"—D'Artagnan held up a hand—"and watch." He walked to the fireplace and softly called to the cat.

Serendipity's ears perked up and she turned away from Christian and walked to the fireplace.

D'Artagnan moved when she neared so that she had to turn around to face him. The cat meowed.

Christian stared at Serendipity, and remained frozen in place.

D'Artagnan urged the cat to turn around again, then patted a finger on the fireplace front.

The cat began to paw at the marble edging of the fireplace.

Aramis moved closer and stared at D'Artagnan. "So, are you trying to tell us that all those times you've been lazing around in the gardens petting this animal, you two have actually been conversing?"

D'Artagnan smiled. "Let's just say we like and understand each other."

Serendipity meowed again, then glanced over her shoulder at Christian.

He swallowed hard and moved slowly toward the cat. "What . . . what are you doing?"

"Okay," D'Artagnan said, watching Christian approach. "We've got him moving in the right direction." He looked at Porthos, still standing near the bed. "Come here and place the cat on the mantel, but try and make it look as if she jumped up."

Porthos nodded. A moment later his large, strong hands wrapped around Serendipity's middle. "Come on, kitty," he said, and swooped her up to the mantel.

Christian froze at the cat's sudden leap.

"*Bon Dieu*," Porthos said, watching him. "The man is probably scared of his own shadow. And to think, he's the one we wanted Brianne to marry. Agh." His face screwed up into a look of utter disgust.

"Hmm. Porthos, gently place the cat's paw on

Never Alone

the medallion," D'Artagnan said, indicating the delicately carved wooden rose on the corner of the mantel. "Then twist it slightly and push it first to the left, then forward with her so the hidden drawer will open."

"Ah!" Aramis said. "It will look like the cat did it accidentally."

D'Artagnan smiled. *"Oui."*

A moment later the secret cavity that had not been opened in three hundred years popped into sight.

"Voilà!" Porthos said.

"Well done, *ma petite*," D'Artagnan said to the cat.

She leaped from the mantel and walked toward the door.

Porthos hurried to allow her exit.

Christian reached into the small drawer that had suddenly appeared from within the fireplace mantel. His heart was racing a hundred miles an hour. He'd found it. He had found the Musketeers' treasure.

His hand came out of the drawer with nothing but a piece of rolled-up parchment. He stared at it, confused. "No," he said, shaking his head and shoving his hand back into the small drawer. "There has to be more. Jewels. Gold. There has to be."

But there was nothing else in the drawer.

Christian yanked away the narrow red ribbon that had been tied around the parchment and held the paper up before him. His eyes quickly scanned the words written so long ago.

"A confession?" he asked a few minutes later. Too angry for words, he threw the parchment to the floor and stormed from the room.

"I don't think our treasure was quite the type he had in mind," Aramis mused.

D'Artagnan smiled as Porthos scooped the parchment from the floor and tucked it under his cloak. "I think we'd best get downstairs and make certain Athos doesn't run his sword through Brianne's young man."

"But he betrayed her," Porthos said. "You can't mean to let him stay."

"I think that's up to her," D'Artagnan said. "But if he's a corpse, she won't have much of a choice, will she?"

They had almost reached the study when they heard Brianne's scream.

SEVENTEEN

Startled by Brianne's scream, Athos froze, his sword in midair, and whirled to face her.

Mace did the same.

She felt light-headed as her gaze darted nervously back and forth between the two men while she struggled against the disbelief threatening to overwhelm her. Her eyes finally settled on Mace. "You . . . you can see him," she said.

Mace tore his gaze from hers and looked back at Athos.

The blond, bewhiskered Musketeer lowered his sword and glowered at Mace.

That was when D'Artagnan, Aramis, and Porthos burst through the bookshelf wall. Mace jerked around at their entrance and stared at them, clearly shocked. "Who . . . what . . . ?"

"You can see them," Brianne said. Her hands trembled. "You can see them."

Mace looked back at Brianne, shock, disbelief, amazement etched upon his handsome features. "They're . . . real."

"Well, of course we're real," Porthos snapped, indignant.

Aramis looked at him and sneered. "He means, he can see us."

"But how?" Brianne asked softly.

"Brianne, Brianne," Mrs. Peel called. She pushed past Felix and ran to Brianne. "He's related."

Brianne turned to her, clearly shocked. "What? Related to whom?"

"Aramis."

"What?" Aramis growled. "Who?"

Mrs. Peel pressed a hand to her heaving chest and took a deep breath, trying to calm herself.

"Here, sit down," Brianne said, guiding the elderly housekeeper to a chair.

Mrs. Peel flopped down and they all gathered around her, eager to hear what she had to say.

Except for Mace. He propped a hip on Brianne's desk and stared at the sword in his hand. He'd been fencing with a ghost. A man who'd lived and died over three hundred and fifty years before. It was impossible.

He looked back up at Brianne.

She stood over Mrs. Peel, two Musketeers standing on either side of her. Felix hovered behind the older woman.

As if feeling his gaze on her, Brianne looked over her shoulder at him.

Their eyes met and held for a long moment, then she turned back to the housekeeper. "Okay, say it slowly," Brianne said.

Mrs. Peel nodded. "I was in the library the other night, getting one of Mr. St. John's journals for him. It was up on one of the upper shelves. I was going to get John to come in and climb the ladder, but I knew he was busy out in the potting shed so—"

"You didn't go up that ladder yourself?" Brianne said.

"Yes, and I knocked several books down too. Anyway"—Mrs. Peel waved a dismissing hand—"that's when I saw it."

"What?" everyone asked.

"The picture. One of the old books fell open, and when I finally got my big ol' body down off that ladder and went to pick it up, I couldn't believe what I was looking at."

"What?" everyone asked again, the sound of exasperation echoing through the room.

"His picture." She pointed at Mace.

"My picture?" He pushed away from the desk and stood.

Mrs. Peel shook her head. "Well, not his picture exactly. His great-grandfather seven times removed."

Mace stared, dumbfounded.

Felix made an impatient noise in his throat,

then moved around where he could see her face. "So, some old ancestor of his was in one of the history books, or someone that looked like him. So what?"

Mrs. Peel shook her head again. "They looked too much alike for it to be coincidence, and the picture in the book was of Aramis's great-grandson."

"My great-grandson?" Aramis bellowed.

"Well, you know my daughter dabbles in that genealogy stuff, Miss Brianne, so I called her, and that was her calling me back a few minutes ago."

Felix moved away from the others and hurried to the library.

Brianne straightened and turned to look at Mace. "You knew this?" she asked, her tone hard and steady.

His brows shot up. "Knew what?"

She looked back at Mrs. Peel.

"He's Aramis's grandson, nine times removed," the housekeeper said.

"I'm what?" Mace exclaimed.

"So he's French," D'Artagnan said, nodding and sounding quite satisfied.

"I knew I liked him," Porthos said, and laughed.

Felix walked back in with the book in question open in his hands. "She's right," he announced.

The others turned to look at him as he approached.

He held the book out, the page opened to the

picture. Brianne looked at the portrait of Richard Aramis Moret, then turned to look at Mace. Except for the clothes and the hairstyle, it was almost a mirror image of him.

The shock on her face told him everything, but he had to see for himself. He strode to Felix's side and looked at the book, then shook his head. "I don't believe this. No one in my family ever said—"

"Well, isn't that just dandy," Aramis snapped, drawing everyone's attention. "My own descendants don't even remember me."

Mace turned to stare at the darkly handsome Musketeer.

Athos moved quietly to Brianne's side. "You want him to stay now?" he whispered softly.

The question reminded her of why she'd been upset with Mace earlier. He had deceived her. No matter what else had happened, that fact still remained. He had come to LeiMonte seeking a way to aide in his client's takeover of St. John Shipping, and he had used her in the process.

Tears stung the back of her eyes and she fought them away. There was a rending deep within her chest as she struggled against the desire to reach out to him and beg him to say it wasn't so. But it *was* so. She couldn't deny that. Brianne straightened her shoulders and pushed the traitorous feelings away.

There would be time for tears later, in the privacy of her room.

The moment she turned toward him and he saw her eyes, Mace knew he was about to lose the woman he loved.

"I expect you to be gone within the hour, Mr. Calder," Brianne said, her tone laced with ice.

"You're throwing out a member of my family!" Aramis said indignantly.

"A family snake," Athos said.

Brianne looked at Aramis. "I'm sorry," she said softly. She started to turn away, then paused and looked back at Mace. "You can tell Mr. Melanstrup that he will not be acquiring St. John Shipping, unless he wants the fight of his life."

Everyone remained silent, watching.

"Brianne, please," Mace said. He moved to her, reached for her arms, but she stepped away from him.

Suddenly everything he'd ever held important didn't matter. If he lost her, he knew nothing would ever be important to him again.

When Jaclyn had told him it was over, he'd found he hadn't really cared that much. His ego had been bruised, but that was all. When Stephanie had broken their engagement, he'd been angry, but only because she'd been so public about it. And again, his ego had been bruised.

But the idea of never seeing Brianne again, of never holding her in his arms again, making love to her again . . . Mace felt as if his heart was being ripped from his chest. As if his soul's very existence was threatened. "You have to listen to me. I didn't know when I came here that I'd fall in love with you. This was just another job. I didn't . . ."

The words struck her heart like a dagger, and she nearly reeled under the pain. They were the words she'd waited her entire life to hear . . . words she'd thought would make her the happiest woman on earth . . . words that only a few hours earlier she'd dreamed of hearing from his lips. Fighting to maintain her composure, Brianne met his eyes. "Within the hour, Mr. Calder," she said coldly, and turned away.

A crash suddenly sounded from the foyer, followed by a loud curse, and a cat's howling screech.

Brianne ran for the door. Everyone instantly followed.

Christian sat sprawled at the bottom of the staircase.

Serendipity stood in the middle of the foyer looking indignant.

A suitcase lay open halfway down the stairs, Christian's once neatly packed clothes having fallen out in a heap.

Brianne hurried to Christian. "What happened?"

"That cat!" Christian spat, pointing at Serendipity. "I was coming down the stairs, and it ran right between my legs and tripped me."

"Oh, I'm so sorry," Brianne said.

"Way to go, kitty," Porthos said, and laughed.

Brianne shot him an admonishing glance, then

turned back to Christian. "Are you leaving?" she asked, eyeing his suitcase.

D'Artagnan leaned toward Porthos. "Check out his valise," he said softly. "See if there's anything in there that shouldn't be."

Porthos nodded and moved to the stairs where Christian's suitcase lay open.

"Yes, I . . ." Christian looked around nervously. "I have some unexpected business to attend to. It just came up. Sorry." He struggled to his feet with Brianne's help.

Porthos slid his hand through the suitcase's tumbled contents. He pulled the rolled parchment from beneath one of the man's crisp, white shirts. "Aha," he said, holding it up. "Obviously he decided it *was* worth something."

Christian stared at the rolled and beribboned parchment as it floated up from his suitcase and hovered in midair over the stairs.

Mace watched like a man in a trance, still unable to believe what he was seeing.

"What is that?" Felix demanded.

Brianne moved away from Christian, who was now clutching the newel post, and mounted the stairs to Porthos's side. He unfurled the parchment and handed it to her. "We hid this in your room a long time ago," he said softly. "About three hundred and eighty years ago, to be exact."

Brianne hurriedly read the words written on the old parchment in an elegant scrawl. She stared at the signature, then looked back up at Porthos.

"This is real? Cardinal Richelieu actually signed this?"

"We didn't give him much of a choice," D'Artagnan said.

She looked back down at the document.

"What is it?" Felix demanded impatiently.

She glanced down at her uncle. "Richelieu's confession that he'd planned and tried to kill the king, Louis."

Felix glared at Christian. "And you were trying to steal it." He turned to Mrs. Peel. "Amelia, call the police."

Mrs. Peel hurried toward the phone, only to see that Mace was already using it.

"Mr. Melanstrup, please," Mace growled into the receiver.

At hearing him, Brianne looked up.

"Donald, this is James Calder. Yes, I am still at LeiMonte. No, I'm not calling to give you an update, I'm calling to say I quit. Yes, you heard right. I quit."

The room seemed eerily still.

"Fine, so ruin me," Mace snapped, and slammed the phone down. Tears shimmered in Brianne's eyes and he prayed that it was because she was happy about what he'd just done. He didn't know any other way to prove to her how much he loved her.

Mace closed the distance between them. "If you can't forgive me, then at least believe that I love you," he said softly.

"Believe him," Aramis said over Mace's shoulder.

Mace glanced at his long-dead ancestor. "Thank you." He turned and moved back down the stairs to Felix. "We have a lot of work to do if we're going to stop Melanstrup from a hostile takeover, Mr. St. John."

Felix smiled, devilment dancing in his old eyes. He rubbed his hands together. "Well, what are we waiting for?" he said gleefully. "I've always loved a good fight."

"All for one," Aramis yelled, drawing his sword and raising it high in the air.

Mace turned back to look at the Musketeers, flanking Brianne on the stairs, swords drawn.

As he'd done only a short while earlier, Athos was suddenly holding the sword from the study and tossed it down, hilt first, to Mace. Mace caught it and raised it in the air toward them. "And one for all," he said.

EIGHTEEN

Brianne stared in the tall mirrors set into the front doors of her armoire and smiled.

"You are happy, *cher ange*?" Porthos asked, suddenly materializing at her side.

D'Artagnan, Aramis, and Athos instantly appeared on her other side.

"How could she not be?" Aramis said. "She is going to marry my great-grandson." He waved a hand. "Nine times removed."

Brianne turned to them. "Yes," she said softly. "I am very happy."

"Then we are happy," Athos said.

"And it is time to go," D'Artagnan reminded them.

Brianne took one last glance in the mirror. She was wearing her mother's wedding dress, a swirl of white silk, satin, and lace, with tiny white seed pearls sewn across the plunging neckline.

Music drifted into the room from its open windows.

"Brianne," D'Artagnan said, "it's time to go." He smiled slyly. "Unless you've changed your mind?"

"Never," Aramis thundered, suddenly indignant.

Brianne smiled. "Never."

"Then it is time," D'Artagnan said.

Aramis helped her lower her veil.

Athos picked up the bouquet of white gardenias from the bed and handed them to her. Their heady perfume immediately filled her lungs.

Aramis stepped before her and, sliding his Musketeer's ring from his finger, lifted her right hand and slid it onto her middle finger. He leaned forward and brushed his lips tenderly across her cheek. "Something borrowed," he said softly, and stepped aside.

Athos took his place. Reaching into his pocket, he retrieved a blue pearl bracelet he'd taken from Charlotte's room earlier. He fastened it around Brianne's wrist. "Something blue." He kissed her other cheek.

Porthos nudged Athos aside and, pulling one of the white plumes from his hat, tucked it into the bouquet of gardenias she held. "Something whimsy," he said, smiling, and kissed her forehead.

"And something new," D'Artagnan said as Porthos stepped aside. He tucked a delicate white lace handkerchief into her hand. "I had Felix pick it up in town." His lips brushed her cheek just as a tear slid over it.

Brianne blinked rapidly, trying to hold back the flood of tears suddenly stinging at her eyes. "I love you all desperately, you know."

They whipped their plumed hats from their heads and all four bowed gracefully.

"The feeling is quite mutual," D'Artagnan said as they straightened.

The sounds of the music grew louder.

"And Felix will have an exorcist out here to send us on our way if we don't get downstairs now," D'Artagnan said, and laughed.

The four Musketeers instantly disappeared.

Brianne gathered her skirts and walked down the hallway toward the stairs.

Mace saw her pause on the threshold of the parlor's French doors and caught his breath.

Brianne trembled with happiness. They'd beaten Donald Melanstrup at his own game, and St. John Shipping was secure. Broadelay Shipping had been acquired, the two men who had deserted Felix because of her appointment as head of the company had found themselves the only mutineers in the whole company . . . and she was more in love than she'd ever thought possible.

Felix, dressed in a white tuxedo, joined Brianne, and as she slipped her arm around his they crossed the terrace and descended the steps to the garden.

The three hundred guests seated in the garden turned in their chairs as Felix and Brianne began their walk down the aisle toward where Mace stood waiting.

Brent Calder, acting as best man for his older brother, leaned toward Mace. "You sure about this?" he whispered, one corner of his mouth curving into a smile.

Mace refused to take his eyes off of Brianne. "More than I've ever been about anything."

Halfway down the aisle, Brianne hesitated. "Where are they?" She looked around, suddenly alarmed.

"Right here, milady," the four Musketeers said, suddenly materializing at the end of the aisle between her and Mace. Athos and Aramis stood on the left of the aisle, facing Porthos and D'Artagnan, who stood on the right.

They drew their swords and held them high, silver blades glistening in reflection of the bright afternoon sun, their tips crossed overhead, creating an arch for her to pass beneath.

Brianne's heart felt near to bursting with joy as she and Felix proceeded to walk toward them. As she passed beneath the swords she paused for just a second and smiled. "All for one," she whispered softly.

"And one for all," the Musketeers responded.

She kissed Felix, then reached out for Mace's hand. His fingers closed, strong and warm, around hers.

EPILOGUE

Her scream awoke everyone in the house, and then some.

Mace bolted out of bed, his heart slamming wildly against his chest, and whirled around to look at his wife.

Felix nearly hit the floor as he struggled to untangle himself from his covers.

Mrs. Peel, whose side of the bed was against the wall of the small bedroom in their cottage behind the main house, frantically climbed over her husband, accidentally giving him a heel in the stomach on the way.

And for a split second D'Artagnan, Athos, Aramis, and Porthos thought King Louis's mother Marie de Médicis had returned to exact vengeance upon them for helping to dethrone her.

Serendipity, who had been asleep on the end of Brianne's bed, was the only one who remained calm. She merely opened one green eye to look at her mistress.

"It's time," Brianne said, gasping softly as a milder pain struck.

"Time?" Mace echoed. His confusion cleared instantly as he stared at her. "Time!" he yelled, and grabbed for his clothes.

Felix pounded on the door. "Brianne?"

Mrs. Peel charged up the stairs.

The four Musketeers suddenly appeared. "What's wrong?" Aramis demanded.

"It's time," Mace said, dancing into his jeans.

"Brianne?" Felix yelled, pounding on the door again.

Mrs. Peel shoved her master key into the lock, opened the door, and pushed past Felix into the room.

"It's time," Brianne said, holding her stomach and reaching for her robe.

"I'll get the car," Porthos yelled, and grabbed Mace's keys from his bureau.

Mace looked up, startled. "No!"

"I've got her suitcase," D'Artagnan said, grabbing the valise Brianne had packed months before.

"We've got Brianne," Aramis said as he and Athos each took one of her arms.

"I've got Brianne," Mace called, shoving them aside.

"Fine," Aramis said, "but just remember . . ."

"Yes, I know," Mace said. "If anything happens to her, I'm dead."

"Right," Athos said.

"Owwww!" Brianne yelled as another pain hit her.

Mace froze. "Another labor pain?"

"No," Felix said sarcastically. "She's howling at the moon. Of course it was a labor pain!"

They moved down the hall, then the stairs, each man still sniping at the other.

"Will you two stop your grumbling and just move it?" Mrs. Peel said.

"Yes, you're upsetting Brianne," Aramis chided.

The two men glared at him.

Brianne was too busy huffing rhythmically to bother with a response.

Mrs. Peel hurried to open the front door.

"Be careful," D'Artagnan said as Brianne stepped over the threshold.

"Hold on to her," Athos urged.

A loud crash sounded from the drive, followed instantly by the careening wail of a car horn.

"Oh, great." Mace groaned.

The front of his black Lexus was scrunched up against one of the giant live-oak trees that bordered the entry drive. Steam was rising from beneath the buckled hood.

Porthos suddenly materialized in front of them. He grinned sheepishly and shrugged. "Sorry, it kind of got away from me."

"Sorry?" Mace snapped.

The other Musketeers glared at their cohort.

Mace looked at Brianne's little sports car. She'd

stopped driving it several months earlier when she had gotten too big to maneuver into the low-slung seat. Felix didn't drive, preferring to call for a cab or limo whenever he needed to go somewhere. That left Mace's pickup. "My truck keys are upstairs," he said.

"Take mine," John Peel said.

His wife beamed up at him as he handed their keys to Mace.

Two hours later Samantha St. John Calder's scream of arrival filled the hospital's delivery room.

"Well, she has a powerful set of lungs," Porthos said, laughing.

"And she's beautiful," Aramis cooed, bending over the baby, who was cradled in a nurse's arms. "Look, I think she has my eyes."

Samantha's little clenched hands smacked against the nurse's breast. "Strong-willed," D'Artagnan said.

Athos smiled wistfully. "Beautiful beyond words."

Startled, Mace looked from one Musketeer to the next. "What are you doing in here?" he whispered harshly.

The nurse glanced over at him. "Pardon?"

He smiled. "Nothing."

"Why shouldn't we be in here?" Porthos challenged.

"Because it's a delivery room," Mace snapped under his breath.

"Excuse me?" the nurse said.

Mace smiled.

"I'm the only one who's supposed to be in here," he said after the woman turned away from him.

"Why?" all four asked in unison.

"I'm the father," Mace replied.

The nurse turned again and smiled. "Yes, we know," she said, looking at Mace as if he were simpleminded.

"That does it," Felix said with a growl, barging into the room. "I'm the only one waiting out there. What's going on?"

Mace threw his arms into the air. "Come on in, Uncle Felix, everyone else has."

"Mr. St. John," one of the nurses said, "I'm afraid—"

"Well, don't be." Felix cut her off. "I don't bite, and I'll have you know I contribute heavily to this hospital."

Brianne smiled.

The nurse placed Samantha in her arms.

Brianne looked at the doctor and nurses. "Can we have just a moment alone?"

The medical team filed out of the room.

Brianne looked across the room at the men in her life and smiled. How had she ever gotten so lucky? "Come here, all of you," she said softly, "and say hello to Samantha."

They crowded around the bed.

Mace touched Samantha's hand and felt a swell of emotion almost overwhelm him when her tiny fingers curled around his outstretched one.

Felix reached out a gnarled hand and tenderly brushed the back of his knuckles against one of Samantha's cheeks. "She's beautiful," he said quietly, and looked at Brianne. "Just like you."

Brianne grasped his hand warmly.

"But will she be able to see us?" D'Artagnan asked, a deep frown creasing his brow.

"Her eyesight won't really be developed for a while," Brianne explained.

"Of course she'll be able to see us," Porthos said, as if the mere thought that she wouldn't was ridiculous.

"It doesn't matter," Athos decided. "We will protect her forever whether she knows we're here or not."

Aramis leaned forward, his face close to the baby's, and stared into her eyes. "How long before we'll know?" he asked.

As if in answer, Samantha gurgled happily as her tiny fingers curled around the end of his goatee and tugged softly.

THE EDITORS' CORNER

The heat is on and nowhere is that more evident than right here at Loveswept. This month's selections include some of our most romantic titles yet. Take one mechanic, one television talk-show host, a masseuse, and a travel agent, then combine them with strong, to-die-for heroes, and you've got yourself one heck of a month's worth of love stories.

Loveswept favorite Mary Kay McComas returns with **ONE ON ONE, LOVESWEPT #894**. Mechanic Michelin Albee has no idea what she's getting into when she picks up stranded motorist Noah Tessler on a lonely stretch of desert highway. Noah's purpose in coming to Gypsum, Nevada, is to meet the woman who captured his late brother's heart and gave birth to Eric, Noah's only living relative. Uncharacteristically, Mich takes a liking to Noah. Trusting him more than she's trusted any man in the past few years, she confides in him about her worries for Eric. As

Noah gets closer to both Mich and her son, will he be able to keep his secret? Once again Mary Kay McComas grabs our hearts in a book as deliciously romantic as a bouquet of wildflowers in a teacup!

In Kathy Lynn Emerson's latest contribution, we learn that love is best when it's **TRIED AND TRUE**, LOVESWEPT #895. Because Vanessa Dare has more than a passing interest in history, she agrees to produce a documentary about professor Grant Bradley's living history center in western New York. Grant knows that having the television talk-show host on the project will bring him the exposure Westbrook Farm needs, but he's surprised when desire sizzles between them. When Nessa doesn't balk at sacrificing present-day comforts, Grant realizes he just might have found the perfect woman. She's content merely to get away from the pressures of work, and as they play the part of an 1890s courting couple, the sweet hunger that transpires could prove to be their destiny. As riveting as the pages of a secret diary, Kathy Lynn Emerson's delectable story of love's mysteries and history's magic is utterly charming.

Donna Kauffman is at her best when she gives us a witty romp, and **TEASE ME**, LOVESWEPT #896, is nothing less. Tucker Morgan knows that his life needs a change. He's just not so sure that posing as a masseur is a change for the better. But since he promised his aunt Lillian he'd investigate the shady goings-on at her Florida retirement community, he'd better take a serious look at those instructional videos she gave him. Sent in to evaluate the new masseur's skills, Lainey Cooper knew she was in trouble from the moment he touched her. If his magical hands turned her knees to mush, Lord knew what he could do to the rest of her body! Aunt Lillian is sure something's happening at Sunset Shores, and insists Lainey and

Tucker team up to uncover its secrets . . . and if a little romance is thrown in on the side, hey, what more can an elderly aunt ask for her nephew? Donna Kauffman delivers a sparkling tale of equal parts mystery and matchmaking.

Welcome Suzanne McMinn, who makes her Loveswept debut with **UNDENIABLE**, LOVESWEPT #897. After his wife left him stranded with four daughters to raise, Garth Holloway decided he wasn't going to add any more women to his life. And when his pretty neighbor Kelly Thompson popped out of a Halloween casket, scaring his youngest child nearly to death, he knew his decision was right. Kelly isn't going to argue with him. She's through with raising children. With her younger siblings now in college, she's free to go wherever her heart desires. But when an undeniable passion reigns, Garth and Kelly can't stay away from each other. His children adore her, not to mention the family dog. Garth doesn't want to hold her back, but faced with unconditional love, will Kelly grab her passport or surrender her solo ticket for a hunk on the family plan? Suzanne McMinn's tale of dreams deferred and temptations tasted is as heartwarming as it is irresistible.

Happy reading!

With warmest wishes,

Susann Brailey *Joy Abella*

Susann Brailey　　　　　　　Joy Abella
Senior Editor　　　　　　　　Administrative Editor

P.S. Look for these women's fiction titles coming in July! Deborah Smith returns with **WHEN VENUS FELL**. A novel of two sisters, seeking refuge from their troubled past, who find love and acceptance amid the shattered remains of a tight-knit family in the mountains of Tennessee. From nationally bestselling author Kay Hooper comes **FINDING LAURA**, now available in paperback. A collector of mirrors, struggling artist Laura Sutherland stumbles across an antique hand mirror that lands her in the midst of the powerful Kilbourne family and a legacy of deadly intent. And fun and laughter abound in **FINDING MR. RIGHT** by Bantam newcomer Emily Carmichael. A femme fatale must return to Earth to find the right man for her best friend. The trouble is, when you're a Welsh corgi, there's only so much you can do to play matchmaker! And immediately following this page, preview the Bantam women's fiction titles on sale in July.

For current information on Bantam's women's fiction, visit our website at the following address:
http://www.bdd.com/romance

Don't miss these exciting
novels from Bantam Books!

On sale in June:

GENUINE LIES
by *Nora Roberts*

THE HOSTAGE BRIDE
by *Jane Feather*

THE WEDDING CHASE
by *Rebecca Kelley*

Genuine Lies
BY NORA ROBERTS

She was a legend. A product of time and talent and her own unrelenting ambition. Eve Benedict. Men thirty years her junior desired her. Women envied her. Studio heads courted her, knowing that in this day when movies were made by accountants, her name was solid gold. In a career that had spanned nearly fifty years, Eve Benedict had known the highs, and the lows, and used both to forge herself into what she wanted to be.

She did as she chose, personally and professionally. If a role interested her, she went after it with the same verve and ferocity she'd used to get her first part. If she desired a man, she snared him, discarding him only when she was done, and—she liked to brag—never with malice. All of her former lovers, and they were legion, remained friends. Or had the good sense to pretend to be.

At sixty-seven, Eve had maintained her magnificent body through discipline and the surgeon's art. Over a half century she had honed herself into a sharp blade. She had used both disappointment and triumph to temper that blade into a weapon that was feared and respected in the kingdom of Hollywood.

She had been a goddess. Now she was a queen with a keen mind and keen tongue. Few knew her heart. None knew her secrets.

Julia wasn't certain if she'd just been given the world's most fascinating Christmas present or an enormous lump of coal. She stood at the big bay window of her Connecticut home and watched the wind hurl the snow in a blinding white dance. Across the room, the logs snapped and sizzled in the wide stone fireplace. A bright red stocking hung on either end of the mantel. Idly, she spun a silver star and sent it twirling on its bough of the blue spruce.

The tree was square in the center of the window, precisely where Brandon had wanted it. They had chosen the six-foot spruce together, had hauled it, puffing and blowing, into the living room, then had spent an entire evening decorating. Brandon had known where he'd wanted every ornament. When she would have tossed the tinsel at the branches in hunks, he had insisted on draping individual strands.

He'd already chosen the spot where they would plant it on New Year's Day, starting a new tradition in their new home in a new year.

At ten, Brandon was a fiend for tradition. Perhaps, she thought, because he had never known a traditional home. Thinking of her son, Julia looked down at the presents stacked under the tree. There, too, was order. Brandon had a ten-year-old's need to shake and sniff and rattle the brightly wrapped boxes. He had the curiosity, and the wit, to cull out hints on what was hidden inside. But when he replaced a box, it went neatly into its space.

In a few hours he would begin to beg his mother to let him open one—just one—present tonight, on Christmas Eve. That, too, was tradition. She would refuse. He would cajole. She would pretend reluctance. He would persuade. And this year, she thought, at last, they would celebrate their Christmas in a real home. Not in an apartment in downtown Manhattan, but a house, a home, with a yard made for snowmen, a big kitchen designed for baking cookies. She'd so badly needed to be able to give him all this. She hoped it helped to make up for not being able to give him a father.

Turning from the window, she began to wander around the room. A small, delicate-looking woman in an oversized flannel shirt and baggy jeans, she always dressed comfortably in private to rest from being the scrupulously groomed, coolly professional public woman. Julia Summers prided herself on the image she presented to publishers, television audiences, the celebrities she interviewed. She was pleased by her skill in interviews, finding out what she needed to know about others while they learned very little about her.

Her press kit informed anyone who wanted to know that she had grown up in Philadelphia, an only child of two successful lawyers. It granted the information that she had attended Brown University, and that she was a single parent. It listed her professional accomplishments, her awards. But it didn't speak of the hell she had lived through in the three years before her parents had divorced, or the fact that she had brought her son into the world alone at age eighteen. There was no mention of the grief she had felt when she had lost her mother, then her father within two years of each other in her mid-twenties.

Though she had never made a secret of it, it was far from common knowledge that she had been adopted when she was six weeks old, and that nearly eighteen years to the day after had given birth to a baby boy whose father was listed on the birth certificate as unknown.

Julia didn't consider the omissions lies—though, of course, she had known the name of Brandon's father. The simple fact was, she was too smooth an interviewer to be trapped into revealing anything she didn't wish to reveal.

And, amused by being able so often to crack façades, she enjoyed being the public Ms. Summers who wore her dark blond hair in a sleek French twist, who chose trim, elegant suits in jewel tones, who could appear on *Donahue* or *Carson* or *Oprah* to tout a new book without showing a trace of the hot, sick nerves that lived inside the public package.

When she came home, she wanted only to be Julia. Brandon's mother. A woman who liked cooking her son's dinner, dusting furniture, planning a garden. Making a home was her most vital work and writing made it possible.

Now, as she waited for her son to come bursting in the door to tell her all about sledding with the neighbors, she thought of the offer her agent had just called her about. It had come out of the blue.

Eve Benedict.

Still pacing restlessly, Julia picked up and replaced knickknacks, plumped pillows on the sofa, rearranged magazines. The living room was a lived-in mess that was more her doing than Brandon's. As she fiddled with the position of a vase of dried flowers or the angle of a china dish, she stepped over kicked-off shoes, ignored a basket of laundry yet to be folded. And considered.

Eve Benedict. The name ran through her head like magic. This was not merely a celebrity, but a woman who had earned the right to be called star. Her talent and her temperament were as well known and as well respected as her face. A face, Julia thought, that had graced movie screens for almost fifty years, in over a hundred films. Two Oscars, a Tony, four husbands—those were only a few of the awards that lined her trophy case. She had known the Hollywood of Bogart and Gable; she had survived, even triumphed, in the days when the studio system gave way to the accountants.

After nearly fifty years in the spotlight, this would be Benedict's first authorized biography. Certainly it was the first time the star had contacted an author and offered her complete cooperation. With strings, Julia reminded herself, and sunk onto the couch. It was those strings that had forced her to tell her agent to stall.

She thrilled with her "V" series. She dazzled with her "Charm Bracelet" trilogy. Now, following nine consecutive national bestsellers, Jane Feather takes on readers' favorite topic with the first novel in an enthralling "bride" trilogy.

The Hostage Bride
BY *JANE FEATHER*

Bride #1 is the outspoken Portia. . . . It's bad enough that seventeen-year-old Portia Worth is taken in by her uncle, the marquis of Granville, after her father dies. As the bastard niece, Portia knows she can expect little beyond a roof over her head and a place at the table. But it truly adds insult to injury when the Granville's archenemy, the outlaw Rufus Decatur, hatches a scheme to abduct the marquis's daughter—only to kidnap Portia by accident. Portia, who possesses more than a streak of independence as well as a talent for resistance, does not take kindly to being abducted—mistakenly or otherwise. Decatur will soon find himself facing the challenge of his life, both on the battlefield and in the bedroom, as he contends with this misfit of a girl who has the audacity to believe herself the equal of any man. . . .

"Now just who do we have here?"

Portia drew the reins tight. The quivering horse raised its head and neighed in protest, pawing the ground. Portia looked up and into a pair of vivid blue eyes glinting with an amusement to match the voice.

"And who are you?" she demanded. "And why have you taken those men prisoner?"

Her hood had fallen back in her struggles with the horse and Rufus found himself the object of a fierce green-eyed scrutiny from beneath an unruly tangle of hair as orange-red as a burning brazier. Her complexion was white as milk, but not from fear, he decided; she looked far too annoyed for alarm.

"Rufus Decatur, Lord Rothbury, at your service," he said solemnly, removing his plumed hat with a flourish as he offered a mock bow from atop his great chestnut stallion. "And who is it who travels under the Granville standard? If you please . . ." He raised a bushy red eyebrow.

Portia didn't answer the question. "Are you abducting us? Or is it murder you have in mind?"

"Tell you what," Rufus said amiably, catching her mount's bridle just below the bit. "We'll trade questions. But let's continue this fascinating but so far uninformative exchange somewhere a little less exposed to this ball-breaking cold."

Portia reacted without thought. Her whip hand rose and she slashed at Decatur's wrist, using all her force so that the blow cut through the leather gauntlet. He gave a shout of surprise, his hand falling from the bridle, and Portia had gathered the reins, kicked at the animal's flanks, and was racing down the track, neither knowing nor caring in which direction, before Rufus fully realized what had happened.

Portia heard him behind her, the chestnut's pounding hooves cracking the thin ice that had formed over the wet mud between the ridges on the track. She urged her horse to greater speed and the animal, still panicked from the earlier melee, threw up his head and plunged forward. If she had given him his head he would have bolted but she hung on, maintaining some semblance of control, crouched low over his neck, half expecting a musket shot from behind.

But she knew this was a race she wasn't going to win. Her horse was a neat, sprightly young gelding, but he hadn't the stride or the deep chest of the pursuing animal. Unless Rufus Decatur decided for some reason to give up the chase, she was going to be overtaken within minutes. And then she realized that her pursuer was not overtaking her, he was keeping an even distance between them, and for some reason this infuriated Portia. It was as if he was playing with her, cat with mouse, allowing her to think she was escaping even as he waited to pounce in his own good time.

She slipped her hand into her boot, her fingers closing over the hilt of the wickedly sharp dagger Jack had insisted she carry from the moment he had judged her mature enough to attract unwelcome attention. By degrees, she drew back on the reins, slowing the horse's mad progress even as she straightened in the saddle. The hooves behind her were closer now. She waited, wanting him to be too close to stop easily. Her mind was cold and clear, her heart steady, her breathing easy. But she was ready to do murder.

With a swift jerk, she pulled up her horse, swinging round in the saddle in the same moment, the dagger in her hand, the weight of the hilt balanced between her index and forefingers, steadied by her thumb.

Rufus Decatur was good and close and as she'd hoped his horse was going fast enough to carry him right past her before he could pull it up. She saw his startled expression as for a minute he was facing her head on. She threw the dagger, straight for his heart.

It lodged in his chest, piercing his thick cloak.

The hilt quivered. Portia, mesmerized, stared at it, for the moment unable to kick her horse into motion again. She had never killed a man before.

"Jesus, Mary, and sainted Joseph!" Rufus Decatur exclaimed in a voice far too vigorous for that of a dead man. He pulled the dagger free and looked down at it in astonishment. "Mother of God!" He regarded the girl on her horse in astonishment. "You were trying to stab me!"

Portia was as astonished as he was, but for rather different reasons. She could see no blood on the blade. And then the mystery was explained. Her intended victim moved aside his cloak to reveal a thickly padded buff coat of the kind soldiers wore. It was fair protection against knives and arrows, if not musket balls.

"You were chasing me," she said, feeling no need to apologize for her murderous intent. Indeed, she sounded as cross as she felt. "You abducted my escort and you were chasing me. Of course I wanted to stop you."

Rufus thought that most young women finding themselves in such a situation, if they hadn't swooned away in fright or thrown a fit of strong hysterics first, would have chosen a less violent course of action. But this tousled and indignant member of the female sex obviously had a rather more down to earth attitude, one with which he couldn't help but find himself in sympathy.

"Well, I suppose you have a point," he agreed, turning the knife over in his hand. His eyes were speculative as he examined the weapon. It was no toy. He looked up, subjecting her to a sharp scrutiny. "I should have guessed that a lass with that hair would have a temper to match."

"As it happens, I don't," Portia said, returning his scrutiny with her own, every bit as sharp and a lot less benign. "I'm a very calm and easy-going person in general. Except when someone's chasing me with obviously malicious intent."

"Well, I have to confess I do have the temper to match," Rufus declared with a sudden laugh as he swept off his hat to reveal his own brightly burnished locks. "But it's utterly dormant at present. All I need from you are the answers to a couple of questions, and then you may be on your way again. I simply want to know who you are and why you're riding under Granville protection."

"And what business is it of yours?" Portia demanded.

"Well . . . you see, anything to do with the Granvilles is my business," Rufus explained almost apologetically. "So, I really do need to have the answers to my questions."

"What are you doing with Sergeant Crampton and his men?"

"Oh, just a little sport," he said with a careless flourish of his hat. "They'll come to no real harm, although they might get a little chilly."

Portia looked over her shoulder down the narrow lane. She could see no sign of either the sergeant and his men or Rufus Decatur's men. "Why didn't you overtake me?" She turned back to him, her eyes narrowed. "You could have done so any time you chose."

"You were going in the right direction so I saw no need," he explained reasonably. "Shall we continue on our way?"

The right direction for what?

In the tradition of *New York Times* bestseller Betina Krahn comes a sparkling new talent with a witty, passionate tale of a spinster wary of desire—and the charming rogue who's determined to change her tune. . . .

The Wedding Chase
BY REBECCA KELLEY

Wolfgang Hardwicke, the Earl of Northcliffe, is up to no good—as usual. So he isn't certain why he rescues the drunken gambler from a fight. And he never expects to be rewarded with a heavenly, all-too-brief glimpse of the gambler's exquisite sister, clad only in her nightgown. Nor does he guess that he'll see her again, lighting up a dull party as she plays piano with an unguardedly rapturous expression—an expression Wolfgang would like to see in decidedly different circumstances. . . . Unlike her admirer, Miss Grizelda Fleetwood is an unabashed do-gooder, one who has as soft a heart for her ne'er-do-well brother as for the unfortunates she helps. Though Zel has no interest in matrimony, she's determined to marry to save her family from financial ruin. That is, if she can find a suitable match before the unprincipled and relentless Earl of Northcliffe ruins her reputation . . . or steals her defenseless heart.

Eventually, Wolfgang found himself in the music room. He hadn't practiced in months but, inspired by Miss Fleetwood's performance, he couldn't resist trying his hand. First the pianoforte, then its player.

A smile brushed his lips. Her sweet blush contrasted so intriguingly with her bold behavior. She followed along with his game of cat and mouse, allowing him to sit far too close, moving away only a bit to encourage rather than discourage him. Yet when faced with competition, she deserted the field, leaving him in Isadora's clutches despite his silent plea for aid.

He sighed, seating himself on the bench. If he wished to be an honorable gentleman, any doubts dictated that he leave her alone. But why should he allow a few scruples to interfere with his amusements? And she did amuse him.

He would proceed with flirtation, moving ever so skillfully into seduction. Smiling, Wolfgang rifled through the sheet music arrayed on the pianoforte. Finding a familiar Mozart sonata, he began to softly finger the hardwood keys.

He was thoroughly destroying the piece when he sensed another presence in the room. A spicy scent. Wolfgang turned to see Grizelda Fleetwood, in another dowdy gown, hesitating at the door. He stopped abruptly, surprised at his embarrassment.

"Discovered! The foul deed uncovered!" He smiled, eased the bench back and stood with a flourish. "I confess my guilt. I've murdered Mozart."

She laughed, a throaty sound of full, easy humor that struck a chord within him. Her laughter bore no resemblance to the rehearsed titter affected by the ladies of the *ton*. "I wouldn't call it murder, my lord, maybe a little unintentional mayhem. You have a fine hand, but it's clear you rarely practice."

"The truth is indeed revealed. I seldom, almost never practice. Lacking discipline, I have become a much better listener than player." Wolfgang took a step closer, drawing her eyes to his. "You are quite beyond my touch."

That faint blush appeared again, as she set a well-worn portfolio on the table. "Do you sight read?"

"About as well as I play."

"That will be fine. I have a few Bach pieces my music master arranged for four hands on the pianoforte." Her low voice softened. "The easier part was for my brother. My part acts as the counterpoint. Would you like to try?"

"I would be honored to take instruction." He bowed, sat back on the bench and patted the seat beside him. "But please be kind to your humble pupil, Madam Music Master."

An answering smile lit her face as she opened her portfolio. She pulled out some tattered papers before sitting a respectable distance from him on the bench. He took the music, scanned it quickly and laid it out where they both could see.

Miss Fleetwood removed her eyeglasses, pushed back a wisp of dark brown hair and ran bare fingers lightly over the keys. "Are you ready? My part joins in after the first few measures."

Wolfgang began to tentatively tap out the notes. The piece was easy and his confidence rapidly increased. Soon she joined in, the notes prancing, circling, interlacing playfully. They both reached to turn the page, his hand met hers, skin to skin. A thrumming—a contralto's lowest note—reverberated through him. Their gazes crossed and locked. Suddenly he wanted to touch much more than her fingers. As if he'd spoken the thought aloud, she looked away, stumbling over the next measure. She seemed to draw herself in, her slender form compact and contained, and continued the piece. He inhaled slowly, breathing in her scent, and found his place in the music, barely missing a note.

As they finished the arrangement, she turned to him with what might have been a smile had her mouth not been so tight. "I believe you could be quite good if you applied yourself."

The corner of his lips twitched as he restrained an answering smile. "I'm always good when I apply myself, Miss Fleetwood." The threatening grin broke through. "But speaking of good, you should see me ride. Do you ride?"

"Ride? What do you . . ." She hesitated slightly. "I ride, but not well."

"Good. I've played your student, now you'll play mine."

On sale in July:

WHEN VENUS FELL
by Deborah Smith

FINDING LAURA
by Kay Hooper

FINDING MR. RIGHT
by Emily Carmichael

Bestselling Historical Women's Fiction

ᛞAmanda Quickᛞ

___ 28354-5 SEDUCTION ...$6.50/$8.99 Canada
___ 28932-2 SCANDAL ....$6.50/$8.99
___ 28594-7 SURRENDER ....$6.50/$8.99
___ 29325-7 RENDEZVOUS ....$6.50/$8.99
___ 29315-X RECKLESS ....$6.50/$8.99
___ 29316-8 RAVISHED ....$6.50/$8.99
___ 29317-6 DANGEROUS ....$6.50/$8.99
___ 56506-0 DECEPTION ....$6.50/$8.99
___ 56153-7 DESIRE ....$6.50/$8.99
___ 56940-6 MISTRESS ....$6.50/$8.99
___ 57159-1 MYSTIQUE ....$6.50/$7.99
___ 57190-7 MISCHIEF ....$6.50/$8.99
___ 57407-8 AFFAIR ....$6.99/$8.99

ᛞIris Johansenᛞ

___ 29871-2 LAST BRIDGE HOME ...$5.50/$7.50
___ 29604-3 THE GOLDEN
            BARBARIAN ....$6.99/$8.99
___ 29244-7 REAP THE WIND .....$5.99/$7.50
___ 29032-0 STORM WINDS ....$6.99/$8.99

Ask for these books at your local bookstore or use this page to order.

Please send me the books I have checked above. I am enclosing $____ (add $2.50 to cover postage and handling). Send check or money order, no cash or C.O.D.'s, please.

Name _____

Address _____

City/State/Zip _____

Send order to: Bantam Books, Dept. FN 16, 2451 S. Wolf Rd., Des Plaines, IL 60018
Allow four to six weeks for delivery.
Prices and availability subject to change without notice.

FN 16 6/98

Bestselling Historical Women's Fiction

Iris Johansen

____28855-5 THE WIND DANCER ...$5.99/$6.99
____29968-9 THE TIGER PRINCE ...$6.99/$8.99
____29944-1 THE MAGNIFICENT
            ROGUE ....$6.99/$8.99
____29945-X BELOVED SCOUNDREL .$6.99/$8.99
____29946-8 MIDNIGHT WARRIOR .$6.99/$8.99
____29947-6 DARK RIDER ....$6.99/$8.99
____56990-2 LION'S BRIDE ......$6.99/$8.99
____56991-0 THE UGLY DUCKLING...$6.99/$8.99
____57181-8 LONG AFTER MIDNIGHT.$6.99/$8.99
____10616-3 AND THEN YOU DIE....$22.95/$29.95

Teresa Medeiros

____29407-5 HEATHER AND VELVET .$5.99/$7.50
____29409-1 ONCE AN ANGEL ......$5.99/$7.99
____29408-3 A WHISPER OF ROSES .$5.99/$7.99
____56332-7 THIEF OF HEARTS .....$5.50/$6.99
____56333-5 FAIREST OF THEM ALL .$5.99/$7.50
____56334-3 BREATH OF MAGIC ....$5.99/$7.99
____57623-2 SHADOWS AND LACE ...$5.99/$7.99
____57500-7 TOUCH OF ENCHANTMENT..$5.99/$7.99
____57501-5 NOBODY'S DARLING ...$5.99/$7.99

Ask for these books at your local bookstore or use this page to order.

Please send me the books I have checked above. I am enclosing $____ (add $2.50 to cover postage and handling). Send check or money order, no cash or C.O.D.'s, please.

Name _____

Address _____

City/State/Zip _____

Send order to: Bantam Books, Dept. FN 16, 2451 S. Wolf Rd., Des Plaines, IL 60018
Allow four to six weeks for delivery.
Prices and availability subject to change without notice.

FN 16 6/98